Shadow of the Gun

When Luke Harper rode to the aid of Dr John Meeks he found himself sucked into a whirlpool of murder, gunfights and rustling. Bridgetown was torn in half, with townsfolk to the south struggling to lead decent lives while, to the north, Jake Pedlar had set his sights on a more lucrative venture than his saloons and honkytonks. Backed by gunslingers, he planned to take over the Double M ranch.

Harper intended to ride on, but when the strong-willed woman from the Double M called on him for help he could not refuse. He'd take on this one last job before heading back east. Now he faced a desperate struggle – and only his Peacemaker might keep him alive.

Shadow of the Gun

JACK EDWARDES

A Black Horse Western

ROBERT HALE · LONDON

© Jack Edwardes 2006
First published in Great Britain 2006

ISBN-10: 0-7090-7966-4
ISBN-13: 978-0-7090-7966-8

Robert Hale Limited
Clerkenwell House
Clerkenwell Green
London EC1R 0HT

Typeset by Derek Doyle & Associates, Shaw Heath.
Printed and bound in Great Britain by
Antony Rowe Limited, Wiltshire

CHAPTER ONE

Luke Harper had crossed Main Street of Plainsville and was behind the livery stable when he heard the woman scream. He stopped in his tracks before realizing the sound came from close to the saloon. One of the hurdy-gurdy girls with a customer, he reckoned. She had to belong to the noisiest bunch north of the Rio Grande. He stepped out in the fading light, his plains spurs jingling, aiming to reach the barbershop before the dozen or more cowboys he'd seen ride into town.

Then the scream rang out again, the sound skittering between wooden walls to assault his ears. That sure as hell didn't sound like some saloon girl. He spun around in the dirt. The anguished cry reached him again, closer than he'd first thought. He broke into a run, his boots breaking through the crust of the hardpack, heading for the alleyway he'd passed twenty yards before.

A yard past the corner of the livery stable he slammed his boot into the dirt, swinging himself around on his heel, his eyes searching the shadows. Twenty yards down the alleyway two men held a woman hard against the side of the clapboard building. One of the men had her fair hair around his bunched fist, pulling back the woman's head, his face hard against the side of her neck. The other

5

stood, half turned, tearing at the woman's dress.

Harper's sidearm roared, the sound bouncing between the buildings as wood chips flew two feet above the heads of the two men. There was a scream of fear from the woman as Harper saw the men whirl around, both dropping their hands to their gunbelts.

Harper's sidearm roared again. With a shout from one of them, the two men turned and ran down the alleyway to disappear into the darkness.

For a moment Harper stood still, his arm extended, his sidearm steady, his eyes fixed on the spot where the two men had vanished. Then, satisfied, he lowered his Peacemaker. The woman's sobs continued as he reloaded before easing the weapon back into its holster.

He could make out the woman attempting to cover herself with the remnants of her torn dress, and he waited until she appeared more settled.

'The name's Harper, ma'am,' he called. 'I'm gonna walk down towards you.' He paused. 'But only when you feel fine about that, I mean.' The sobs ceased, and Harper heard the woman suck in a gasping lungful of air. There was a moment's silence. Then she called out, 'One moment, Mr Harper.'

She had the voice of a young woman, and whoever she was, she sure had spirit. Most of the women he'd known would be down in the dirt, swooned away. Harper saw her turn from him, the whiteness of a shoulder showing like alabaster, and he guessed she was still trying to fix her torn dress.

'I've a coat here, ma'am, if it'll help,' he called.

Still he made no move to approach her. He slipped out of his short trail coat and held it in his left hand. The curve of her shoulder disappeared into shadow, and she spoke again. At first her voice trembled, but then, to

Harper's surprise, he detected firmness in her words.

'Yes, I'd like that, Mr Harper.'

He walked towards her, his weight forward, as carefully as he would approach a roped mustang, ready to halt in his tracks at the first sign of her backing off down the alley-way.

'You're safe now, ma'am,' he assured her. Deliberately he kept his voice low and steady. 'Those two varmints'll not be comin' back.'

He was maybe four paces from her when he heard her stifle another sob, as she jerked away from him. He stopped still before he slowly raised his hand to hold up the leather jacket.

'This coat'll cover your dress.' His free hand deftly untied his blue neckerchief. 'The bandanna's clean, ma'am, if it'll help.'

There was a silence and Harper was about to speak again when she turned towards him. In the shadows her face was only a pale orb, but he could see blonde hair strewn across one shoulder. Deliberately, still clutching his bandanna, he took the jacket in both hands and moved forward. He was uncertain whether she could see his face but he managed an encouraging smile. When he was a pace from her she half-turned again, allowing him to drop the jacket onto her shoulders. She turned and her hand touched his briefly as she took his bandanna.

As Harper felt the tension ease, anxious voices rang out from the end of the alleyway. Harper saw the glimmer of lanterns. Townsmen, he guessed, attracted by the gunfire. The woman, too, must have realized what was happening.

'They mustn't see me like this!'

'You stay here, ma'am,' he said. 'I'll stop 'em afore they come closer.'

Without waiting for her answer he strode towards the

bobbing lanterns and the sound of voices, calling out a greeting as he approached the group of men. He reached them a further twenty yards down the alleyway.

'Nothing to get stirred up about!' Harper said. 'Coupla no-goods needed scaring off. Nobody's hurt.'

Ahead of him the townsmen spread themselves across the alleyway barring his way, holding up their lanterns to get a better look at him. In the yellow light Harper saw that two of the men carried long guns. A tall, broad-shouldered man with moustaches, a sheriff's star pinned on his rough blue shirt, stepped closer to Harper. His pistol was held loosely at his side. He looked hard at the Peacemaker on Harper's hip, then directly into Harper's eyes.

'Shooting a cannon like that in Plainsville can bring you lotsa trouble, stranger. I'm askin' you to take out that Peacemaker with your left hand mighty slow, and give it over to the deputy here.'

'An' if I don't?'

If the sheriff made a signal Harper didn't see it, but from the shadows came the sound of a sidearm being cocked.

'Take it easy, Sheriff,' Harper said evenly.

He reached over slowly with his left hand to draw his sidearm from its holster. The deputy stepped forward, his hand out, and Harper held out his Peacemaker, butt first.

'You gonna tell me more about what's goin' on?'

'A woman was being attacked, Sheriff. I chased away a coupla varmints,' Harper said. 'She's still there. But take it easy, she's badly shook up.'

'We'll walk down the alley an' take a look.'

Harper shrugged, and turned on his heel. He retraced his steps, this time flanked by shadowy shapes thrown by the lanterns against the buildings on both sides of the alleyway. The sound of his spurs accompanied the crunch of dirt as the townsmen walked behind him.

Thirty feet down the alleyway he stopped suddenly. In the light thrown by the lanterns he could see his trail coat crumpled in the dirt against the wall of the livery stable. There was no sign of the woman. Harper turned to face the sheriff.

'She was right here a coupla minutes ago.'

'The boys'll take a look 'round.' The sheriff gave an order in an undertone and two of the men broke away from the group. He turned to stare hard at Harper. 'What do folks know you by?'

Harper told him.

'You mind puttin' that coat on, Mr Harper?'

Despite the tense atmosphere, Harper's face broke into a grin.

'You've been places, Sheriff.'

He stepped forward and picked up his coat. For an instant he smelled fresh flowers. Memories of another time and another place tugged somewhere at the back of his mind. He was settling the coat on his shoulders when the two men sent to look around rejoined the group.

'Ain't seen nothing, Mr Bolden,' one of them reported to the sheriff.

'None of you heard the woman's screams?' Harper asked.

The townsmen exchanged glances, all shaking their heads. One of the men spoke up.

'Heard the shots, Sheriff, that's all.'

'How many shots you fired, Mr Harper?'

'Just the two.'

One of the townsmen muttered something that Harper couldn't catch and he saw Bolden nod in response.

'I ain't callin' you a liar, Mr Harper,' Bolden said. 'But I'm gonna ask you to take a walk down the jailhouse.'

'What the hell for?'

Bolden's expression didn't change. 'Reckon you ain't acquainted with the situation 'round these parts. There's trouble in the county, an' I'm makin' damn sure it don't spill over down here. Strangers come into town firing off big Colts an' we get jumpy. You're probably an honest man, but I ain't takin' chances.'

'You just hold on there, Sheriff. I tol' you: there was a woman down here gettin' roughed around by no-goods. I put a coupla slugs above their heads, that's all.'

Bolden turned to the deputy holding Harper's Peacemaker. 'We seen any woman hereabouts, Frank?'

'No, Sheriff.'

'Any two varmints takin' to their heels?'

'No, Sheriff.'

Bolden turned to the group of men. 'OK, Frank Jackson an' me will handle this. I'm obliged to you all.'

The three men stood waiting until the townsmen dispersed. Finally Bolden turned back to Harper. 'The jailhouse ain't bad. In this town you even get a cage of your own.' He gestured with his pistol. 'You gonna start walkin'?'

Bolden unlocked the door of his office and stood back on the boardwalk to allow his deputy to step past him.

'Hold on, Harper, while Frank sets up a couple of lamps.'

The two men paused while Jackson rummaged around for a taper to light the lamps secured in metal brackets to the whitewashed walls. After an initial spurt of light a warm glow spread over a neat room, a pot-bellied black stove in one corner standing opposite a dark wooden desk scarred with burns and splashes of ink. Behind the desk stood a high-backed chair. Other chairs stood around the room. Opposite the doorway where Harper stood, a wooden case, pinned to the wall with heavy metal bolts, showed long guns and sidearms. To the right of the case a door was set in the wall. Harper guessed it led to the cages.

'OK, step in.' Bolden pointed past Harper to the stove. 'Help yourself to coffee.'

'I don't need coffee.'

'Don't get ornery, Harper. Get yourself coffee and sit over there.'

Bolden pointed to the chair in front of the desk. 'I got some questions.'

The sheriff pulled the door shut behind him and walked past Harper to sit behind his desk below an old railroad clock pinned to the wall.

'An' get one for me while you're at it.'

For a moment, Harper didn't move. What the hell was going on here? One minute he was heading for a night in jail, the next he was being asked to pour coffee like some damned trail cook. He blew out air from compressed lips. Aw, what the hell! He'd be riding north come daybreak.

He had more to think about than a small-town lawman intent on showing he ran a quiet town. Pouring coffee for Bolden might even keep him out of jail for the night. He took down a couple of tin mugs from the wooden pegs on the wall, and filled them with the hot black coffee from the battered pot that sat atop the stove.

He turned back to the desk to see Bolden swing around and glance at the clock above his head.

'I'll take Harper's sidearm, Frank.'

The deputy stepped forward and put down the Peacemaker on Bolden's desk. From his pocket he took the slugs he'd emptied from the sidearm, and spilled them on the desk.

11

'Time you got back to that beautiful gal of yourn,' Bolden said.

A big grin split Jackson's face. 'Guess it is, Mr Bolden. I'll say goodnight.'

Bolden was silent until the deputy had left the office, then he lifted mug Harper had placed on the desk.

'Loveliest gal in town, Lucy Jackson. An' all of six years old! A damned shame. Her ma ran off a few months back with some fast-talkin' drummer sellin' shoes. Only fair to give Frank some rope for a while.'

Harper shifted on his seat, feeling the back of his neck beginning to prickle. Who the hell was interested in the deputy's daughter?

'Sheriff, you mind tellin' me what sorta game you're playin'?'

Bolden looked at him for a moment. 'No game, Harper. I got this town tied down tight.' He bared his large teeth in a wolfish smile. 'An' I aim to keep it that way.'

'Coupla *ladinos* attackin' a woman don't bother you?'

'I'll catch up with 'em.'

Harper frowned. 'If you reckon I was bein' straight, why am I here?'

Bolden stared across the desk for a few seconds before he replied. 'I'm guessin' Harper, but you ain't exactly what you seem to be, an' I find that a mite troublin'.'

He glanced down at the number of slugs on his desk. 'An' a feller who reloads soon as he's used his sidearm just makes me want to know more about him, that's all.'

Harper was silent for a few seconds. Then he shrugged. 'Old habit from the army, I guess.' He took a sip of his coffee. 'I'm not gonna bring you any trouble. Come daybreak I'll be riding north to Bridgetown. I got important business there with the doc—'

Harper was interrupted by the door from Main Street

12

being opened. A woman, maybe thirty years old, Harper guessed, was framed in the doorway. She was tall, five feet seven or eight. A grey silk dress showed beneath her long woollen cloak that brushed the floor.

The soft skin of her oval-shaped face appeared to glow in the light thrown by the lamps. Her lips were full. But it was her hair that held Harper's attention, a golden blonde, pinned up beneath her little grey hat in some fancy knot he'd seen women use back East. He knew he'd seen hair that colour only an hour or so before. Then he took a second, deeper look at her. Unusually for someone so fair, her eyes were brown. Bolden and Harper were quickly on their feet.

'Miss Abigail!'

Genuine warmth sounded in Bolden's voice. He moved quickly from behind his desk to cross the office and pick up a wide wooden chair, the only one softened with a seat cushion. He placed it before the desk a few feet from Harper.

He waved a hand in Harper's direction, as the woman sat down, settling her skirts, a woman alone but looking very much at ease in the company of two men. Harper guessed that her calling on Bolden was a regular event.

'This tall *hombre* with a Boston accent he's tryin' to hide, is Mr Luke Harper.' Bolden's hand cut the air. 'This lady, Mr Harper, is Miss Abigail Forrest, the biggest ranch owner around Bridgetown, an' a lady who knows more about the law than I'll ever know!'

Harper gave a half-bow towards the woman.

'Then, ma'am, I guess you know a great deal.'

Abigail Forrest smiled, her full lips curving to show a small dimple in her right cheek.

'You flatter me, Mr Harper, as does Mr Bolden who hopes I'll not ask him again to be the sheriff of

Bridgetown,' she said.

Bolden chuckled as the two men sat down. 'Miss Abigail's known me for too many years I like to remember. She believes I'm bored now Plainsville's got to be so quiet these last five years.'

Harper waited, expecting her to say something about the incident behind the livery stable. Now he'd heard her voice he was sure she was the woman from the alleyway.

Instead, Abigail Forrest raised a delicate eyebrow. 'Do you live in Plainsville, Mr Harper?'

Harper shook his head. Maybe she was too embarrassed to talk about what had happened. If so, that was fine with him. 'Just ridin' through. I'm on my way to Bridgetown.'

Her eyes widened. 'That is most interesting, Mr Harper. I catch the stage at noon tomorrow, but maybe you'd join me at the Majestic for coffee at ten. There's some business I wish to discuss with you.'

Harper hesitated. Maybe he'd been out West too long. Ladies back East, as far as he recalled, left talking business to the menfolk. Then he remembered that Bolden had described her as being the biggest rancher around Bridgetown. He'd made no mention of her husband. Sure, the world was changing fast, but ladies like Abigail Forrest weren't in the habit of inviting strangers to join them for coffee. Maybe she was choosing her own time to mention the incident back of the livery. Another thought occurred to him. Maybe it was best to make something clear.

'I'm not plannin' to wear a sheriff's star, Miss Forrest,' he said.

She shook her head. 'That's not it,' she said.

A minute later, with a flurry of silk skirts, a glimpse of high-buttoned boots, and a hint of fresh flowers, she was gone, leaving the two men, seated once again, looking at each other across the desk.

Bolden snorted. 'You're gonna find out for yourself the trouble they got in Bridgetown. Two young gels got 'emselves murdered these last six months.' Bolden wiped a large-knuckled hand across his mouth. 'I'm warnin' you now, no matter what Abigail Forrest tells you, you start interferin', an' you're gonna end up dead!'

CHAPTER TWO

Harper had been up since dawn, his head buzzing from the whiskey bottle he'd shared the previous night with Bolden. Despite Harper's urging, Bolden had refused to talk about Bridgetown. Harper, he'd said, was going to have to wait until his meeting with Abigail Forrest, adding that decent folks in Bridgetown were damned lucky to have Abigail Forrest on their side.

At midnight, swapping trail yarns, they'd learned they'd both been on McPherson's Ridge at Gettysburg, Harper with the cavalry commanded by General John Buford, Bolden with the infantry of the I Corps' First Division. They drank several times to the memory of their fallen comrades. Later, before throwing themselves onto bunks in adjoining cages, they'd also found several reasons to drink the health of the brave Johnny Rebs who'd faced them, and to damn all wars and politicians.

Several kicks at the bath-house door shortly after dawn had gotten Harper the hot tub which cleared his head. Then it was a stop at the Chinaman's for breakfast, a call on the barber, and a visit to the dry goods store for a new bandanna. By the middle of the morning he was set for his meeting with Abigail Forrest.

The desk clerk at the Majestic, a pale-skinned man from the south was apologetic. He coughed nervously, his eyes dropping to Harper's Peacemaker.

'The gun, Mr Harper, erm. . . .' His voice tailed away, his face red.

Harper unbuckled his gunbelt and handed it to the clerk. 'Which way?'

'Miss Abigail's in the private parlour,' the desk clerk said, clearly relieved. 'Along the hall, and second door on your right.'

A few moments later Harper halted beside an open door. Through it he could see Abigail Forrest, a book on her lap, seated beside a high window overlooking Main Street.

Harper stepped into the room, and she lifted her eyes to look directly at him. She smiled, dimpling her cheek, and gestured to the table beside her.

'Coffee as promised, Mr Harper. Close the door, and join me.'

She saw Harper hesitate, his hand on the doorknob, and laughed aloud.

'I've been ranching for ten years, Mr Harper! A closed door will not ruin my reputation! But I appreciate your good manners.'

His tobacco-brown Stetson in hand, Harper closed the door and crossed the room to sit on the chair placed by the table.

Abigail Forrest lifted the pot from the table and poured coffee into a china cup. 'There's cream and sugar, if you wish.'

'Coffee's just fine.'

He wondered how long she'd take to get around to mentioning the previous night. He was beginning to feel that Abigail Forrest was a lot tougher than she looked.

'How much do you know of Bridgetown?' she said, as she poured coffee for herself, and added a spoonful of sugar.

17

'Not much,' he admitted. The coffee tasted good.

'My father and his great friend Walter Riley brought cattle to this land. My father was not without resources, and settled the Double M. Walter Riley acquired adjoining land, smaller, but still profitable. Bridgetown was established, men prospered, a school was built, families came from the East.'

She turned away from Harper to stare through the window overlooking Main Street. He saw her shake her head slightly as if to dismiss unhappy memories.

'My father died almost ten years ago, two years after my mother. Since when I have run the Double M. My first few years were a struggle, but eventually the Double M prospered again.'

She pressed her lips firmly together. 'Then gold was found to the north of the territory.' She looked back at Harper. 'The town's been cut apart. On one side of the bridge decent people try to live their lives as best they can. On the other, Jake Pedlar preys on the miners with a nest of thieves, gamblers, and whores.'

Startled by her forward language, Harper frowned. 'Where we goin' with this, ma'am? I've told you I'll not wear a badge. I've business in Bridgetown, an' I have to think about that.'

'It's true that the town needs a better sheriff, but for now that is not my first concern.' She put down her cup heavily, rattling the spoon in the saucer. 'I'm being ruined, Mr Harper, and I need help. The ranch hands have been splendid and we've got the cattle away towards the railhead. But I'm sure this is what Pedlar's been waiting for. Until recently he's been content to take what he can from his side of the bridge. Now he's trying to drive me off the Double M. His rustlers have been running off my stock. Violent men attack my ranch hands. One of my men was shot two weeks ago, and may die before long.'

'One thing I do know about your town, ma'am: if anyone can save a man with a gunshot wound, John Meeks can.'

'Doctor John Meeks?' Abigail Forrest was suddenly still.

'That's correct. ma'am. He's—'

'Mr Harper, you've obviously not heard,' she interrupted. 'I'm sorry to be the bearer of bad news. John Meeks is dead. He was killed two weeks ago.'

Harper felt the blood drain from his face. His hand twitched, knocking over his coffee cup. Neither he nor Abigail Forrest paid any attention to the black liquid flowing across the table to drip to the floor.

'How did—?' Harper paused, clearing his throat. 'How was he killed?'

'An accident with a horse. He was out riding, having visited a patient. We think his horse spooked, throwing him from his saddle. His head hit a large rock.'

Harper stood up, and stepped over to the window, his back to Abigail Forrest. John Meeks killed when thrown from a spooked horse? John was the best goddamned man on a horse he'd ever seen. He'd stayed in the saddle when Johnny Reb's guns had opened up with grape and canister. Crazy son of a gun had even ridden up to the line at Battery Wagner telling his colonel he had to be there with the wounded.

Harper reached up to feel the slim package beneath his trail shirt. John's letter had brought him over 2000 miles across the country, by horse, by railroad, by stage, and by horse again. Some folks might say John's death meant his business in Bridgetown was now finished. He didn't see it that way. Maybe John's death was an accident. Maybe not. John hadn't given details, only that he needed Harper in Bridgetown. And that, Harper decided, was where he was damn well going.

He turned back to Abigail Forrest to find that she was gazing up at him, concern showing in her brown eyes.

'Was Dr Meeks kinfolk?'

Harper didn't answer the question. Instead, he stepped back to the table.

'Reckon you're gonna need my help,' he said.

Abigail Forrest's face lit up with delight as Harper put a hand on his chair. Her smile faded abruptly as he turned suddenly, holding a finger to his lips. He crossed the room, taking care not to let his spurs ring. Then he flung open the door.

A man stood outside, his fist raised. Harper's left hand snaked out and grasped the man's wrist, forcing it back. The desk clerk uttered a yelp of pain.

'I was just about to knock!' the clerk spluttered. 'I'll send in more coffee!'

'If I thought you'd been listenin' I'd break your arm!'

Harper let go the man's wrist, shoved him away with a hand to his chest, and closed the door.

'Last thing we need is spies around us,' Harper said. 'Now tell me more about this Jake Pedlar.'

Harper sat easily in his saddle, his grey moving along the trail at a steady lope. At fifty dollars from the livery outside of Cheyenne the horse had proved a good buy. Another thirty dollars for a good saddle, a few dollars for extras, and the whole rig had come in for less than a hundred dollars.

For a moment he wondered how many different horses he'd owned since coming West. Too many, maybe. A fresh breeze ruffled the animal's mane, the air cool, and Harper was glad he'd put on a warmer shirt at the coach station where he'd spent the previous night. Another ten miles of steady riding, and he'd be in Bridgetown. A visit to the bathhouse, a fresh set of clothes, and he'd be ready to call on Abigail Forrest.

She was a handsome woman, no getting away from it, but she sure was something of a puzzle. He'd spent maybe an hour with her, but there'd been no mention of the incident behind the livery stable. And she was unmarried. That was a bigger puzzle. Most of the women in these old frontier towns were married with a couple of brats by the time they were twenty.

Maybe she'd been too busy these last years solving the problems with the ranch to spend time with the young gallants of Bridgetown. Now, Jake Pedlar had brought her problems her cowboys couldn't handle. That didn't surprise him. Cowboys could handle cattle, no matter how tough the job, but when serious shooting started most of them were quick to hightail off to distant places.

Anyways, agreeing to work for Abigail Forrest at the Double M gave him useful cover. Maybe John's death would prove to be an accident. If so, he could ride back to Cheyenne, pick up the railroad, and head back East. But if John had been killed to silence him, or to stop him from some course of action, then someone would have to pay, and he, Harper, would be delivering the bill.

He rounded a bend in the trail, feeling the pressure of the wind shifting on his face. Abruptly, he reined back the grey.

What the hell was all this?

Across the trail and spilling onto the rough ground either side was a line of a dozen men. On each flank a man held a long gun aiming directly at him. His hand dropped to his Peacemaker.

'Hold it right there, Harper! You make a move, an' it'll be the last one!'

The caller was at the centre of the line, dark-skinned enough to be Mexican, but with the angular features of a northern European. He sat astride a big roan, a fancy leather vest over a silk shirt, and silver slathered on his spurs.

Harper looked along the line of men. One, with a scar across his nose, probably from a knife slash, Harper vaguely remembered from the saloon in Plainsville. He'd been tracked from the time he saw Abigail Forrest onto the stage, he realized. Goddamn that clerk at the Majestic! He should have broken his arm when he had the chance.

'Seems you know my name.' he called. 'I've heard about you, Pedlar. You always face one man with twelve of your high-line riders?'

'He's callin' ya cold-footed, Jake,' a man called.

'Shut your mouth, Bart,' Pedlar said. He stood up in his stirrups.

'OK, Harper, take off your gunbelt, and make it real slow. Then you and me are gonna have a little talk.'

'We can talk as we are.'

There was the crack of a long gun as dirt spurted two yards ahead of Harper's grey. To Harper's left there was the ratchet sound of a Winchester being reloaded. For a few seconds, Harper's attention was on controlling his animal as the grey skittered across the ground.

'I ain't tellin' you again, Harper! Now take off your goddamned gunbelt.'

His horse again quiet, Harper dropped his reins and unbuckled his belt. No sense in getting shot before giving himself a chance of riding out of this in one piece. Keeping his eyes on Pedlar, he felt for the big metal buckle at his middle. The two pounds of the Peacemaker pulled away the belt from his waist allowing it to fall behind him across the cantle of his saddle.

'Let's see that belt on the ground.'

Harper reached behind him and pushed at the belt until his Peacemaker fell from the saddle, the heavy sidearm thumping onto the loose soil of the trail.

'Now take out your long gun and throw it on the ground.'

Harper unsheathed his Winchester and tossed it aside.

'OK, Pedlar,' he called. 'What we gonna talk about?'

'We're gonna talk about you, Harper! I wanna know what you're plannin' with that fancy lady at the Double M?'

Harper cursed inwardly. So the hotel clerk had been listening at the door. He must have passed on what he'd heard to Scarred Nose who'd ridden back to Bridgetown ahead of him. If he ever got back to Plainsville, he wouldn't stop at breaking an arm.

'No secret, Pedlar. I gotta job to go to. Miss Abigail Forrest's takin' on extra hands for the big house. I'm just one of 'em.'

Mentally, he estimated the distance between himself and the line of men. If they didn't come closer, he might just have a chance.

'Yeah? An' I s'pose you're gonna be sweepin' out the big house with that cannon of yourn?'

Pedlar threw back his head and laughed loudly at his own wit. Shouts of jeering laughter broke out from the men either side of him.

Harper seized his chance. He dug his spurs into the grey's flanks, one hand on his reins, the other frantically grasping at the knife in his boot top, and bending low over the horse's neck, charged across the space separating him from the line of men.

Horses skittered away, their whinnying cutting the air along with the curses of the men, as Harper's grey hurtled into the line intent on breaking through by sheer force.

He almost made it. Only Pedlar, bringing his animal's head around with a cruel tug of his rein, managed to halt for an instant Harper's headlong charge. It was enough. The men nearest Pedlar were onto Harper, reaching out to haul him from his saddle.

He landed with a bone-crunching fall on the hard ground. A boot lashed out at his wrist sending his knife flying across the ground. Other men slipped from their saddles to surround him, kicking and stomping, as Harper rolled himself into a ball trying to avoid the agony of their sharp-toed boots slamming into his body. He wrapped his arms over his head, his face hard down against his chest, until he was able to roll across the ground.

For one precious moment he was on his knees but then the weight of numbers bore him back flat on the ground again. Blood was in his mouth and throat, the acrid taste mixing with the dirt of the trail. He gagged as yet another boot caught the side of his neck. The figures of the men clustering around him, boots and fists pummelling his body, became a blur, as he began to lose consciousness.

He knew then he'd never get up from the ground. Black and red clouds exploded before his eyes. Jesus Christ! He was about to die on a dusty coach trail in a territory he'd never seen before. His body felt as if it was on fire. His thoughts hurtled into a pit of blackness. The distant bugle call he heard was but the echo of that blood-soaked day on McPherson's Ridge, forever etched into his mind.

CHAPTER THREE

Harper opened his eyes. Above him, rough-hewn timbers pressed on him, only a few inches from his face. For several seconds his thoughts tumbled over each other. What the hell was going on? Then he remembered, and croaked a cry of horror. This was his casket, and he'd been buried while still alive!

Behind the pain he felt in his gut, his innards knotted. He'd heard of men buried before they were dead. A memory flash brought back a casket being trundled through the streets of Boston fitted with a bell, strings leading from its clapper strings through a hole in the screwed down lid.

How long had he been here? How long would it take for the air to seep away? He tried to rise, but heavy material pressed down on his shoulders. He screwed his eyes shut in sheer terror, opening them almost immediately. Death should have taken him on the trail. His breath came in short bursts, agony searing his brain.

The mist in front of his eyes cleared and the timbers receded to some six feet above him. Soil and bunch and buffalo grass were packed between axe-scarred lengths of wood. With a strangled cry of relief Harper realized he was on his back looking up at the roof of a homesteader's cabin. He was alive! His heart hammered against the wall of his chest.

Instinctively, he reached for his Peacemaker, only to find his fingers clutching at the wool of his red Balbriggans beneath the weight of a bedroll that spilled over the edges of the cot on which he lay.

He moved his gunhand again and a shuddering pain shot through the length of his body, searing his chest, hacking at his guts as if he'd been kicked by some ornery mule. Think, goddamnit! Where the hell was he? How long had he been in this bunk? How did he get from being stomped on the coach trail into this cabin? Who had brought him to this place with its dusty gloom lightened only by the rays of the sun penetrating an open square in one of the walls?

'What the hell's goin' on?'

Instead of the intended bellow of rage and confusion Harper's voice was barely a croak. He tried to throw off the bedroll before surrendering to its weight across his body. His head that he'd barely managed to raise from the wooden bunk sank back.

A memory flash sent him back to the days after Gettysburg, the pictures in his mind haunted by blue-coated men, some hobbling around with the aid of rough crutches, others with empty sleeves tied to their sides, all their eyes stained with horror. One rifleman sat with his head in his hands attempting to hide from his comrades the gaping red wound where once his nose had been.

Please God, don't make me spend the rest of my life like that.

An instant explosion of light caused Harper to screw his eyes shut for a second. Sunlight poured into the cabin as the door was thrown open, enabling Harper to see better the interior of the cabin. A rough table and two chairs stood close to a pot-bellied stove. A blackened chimney thrust upwards from the stove to a hole in the timbers of the roof. Beyond the table, rough curtains covered what Harper guessed was another bunk.

Pain stabbed behind his eyes as he turned his head. In the doorway, a tall figure was outlined in sunlight. Dark hair fell to broad shoulders. Unable to make out the man's face, Harper guessed that the man was staring hard in his direction. Ignoring the pain, Harper turned his head again. Maybe his Peacemaker was within reach. As the figure moved towards him Harper could see that he wore a strange suit, the colour of blueberries.

Harper's head fell back to the bunk. Despite the pain that cut to his very bones, he had a wild impulse to laugh aloud. After all he'd been through he was to be finished by a man wearing velvet!

The man halted alongside the cot, bent over and peered into Harper's face. His eyes, Harper saw, were black as coal and sharp as a skinning knife.

'Excellent! You're awake at last,' he said. 'Now tell me your name.'

'Who the hell are you?' Harper croaked.

'A friend in need,' the man said. 'Now tell me your name.'

What the hell! 'Harper. Luke Harper.'

The man, no more than thirty, Harper guessed, nodded vigorously as if a question of momentous importance had been answered correctly.

'Excellent!' It was a word he seemed fond of. 'Now tell me when and where you were born.'

'Listen, stranger. . . .'

The man held up a hand. 'Just answer the question.'

Harper's voice rasped. 'Hell, mister! OK, '38, Concord, Massachusetts. Now tell me who you are!'

Harper's question was ignored.

'Excellent!'

A genuine smile of pleasure appeared on the man's face. 'You're a very lucky man, Mr Harper. And a tough one. No damage to the brain, I'm sure. You've not lost any teeth. No bones broken, and you stopped passing blood three days ago.'

'Are you a doctor?' Harper rasped.

'Indeed not, sir. But I confess I almost took up the leech before I recognized my true calling.' He took a pace backward, bowed, and waved his hand to the corner of the cabin.

'Thomas James Gladwin, of London, England,' he announced. 'Portrait painter in oils to gentlefolk.' He smiled, showing even teeth. 'Those who have money, that is!'

With an effort Harper lifted his head to follow the direction of Gladwin's outstretched hand. In the corner of the cabin he could see a square of rough paper, pinned to wood, and supported on a makeshift stand. Charcoal black lines showed the head and shoulders of a man.

'Mean-looking critter,' Harper rasped.

Gladwin threw back his head and laughed aloud. 'You'll look better without the whiskers,' he said. He examined his work with studied seriousness, and apparently satisfied, nodded. 'A useful exercise to occupy these last few days.'

Harper's head fell back again. 'You gonna tell me where I am?'

'You're a mile back from where you were attacked by those road-agents. A cabin built by the brothers Williams, I've been told. They've gone after gold, so I've moved in for a while.'

Gladwin's face lost its smile. He turned away to carry a chair from the table, and placed it beside Harper's bunk.

'I was in the cottonwoods on the high ground above the trail and saw what was happening,' Gladwin explained.

'The odds seemed a mite unfair, so I decided that you needed help.'

'You tellin' me you took on that trail-trash?'

'Goodness me, nothing of the sort! That was Gabriel's doing.'

Harper was beginning to feel that his head might explode. 'OK, Mr Gladwin. Who the hell is Gabriel?'

Instead of answering, Gladwin stood up, and crossed the cabin to delve into a leather case. Brass glinted in the sunlight as he returned to his chair.

'This is Gabriel, Mr Harper!'

Gladwin held above his head a brass bugle, reflected sunlight flashing from the polished metal. Gladwin lowered his arm, and looked fondly at the instrument.

'Not for the first time did Gabriel save me from a most perilous situation.'

He stood up, took from his pocket a large red and white spotted bandanna, and balling the cloth in calloused fingers, rammed it into the mouth of the bugle. Raising the instrument to his lips he blew with bulging cheeks the first notes of the Cavalry's order to advance.

A grunt of astonishment came from Harper. Only a few feet from the bugle, he could have sworn he was hearing the bugle from maybe a mile away.

Gladwin lowered the bugle, loosened the cloth, and blew the bugle again. This time, the sounds seemed closer, maybe half a mile away. For a third time he blew the bugle, the notes louder, and sounding much closer.

A smile splitting his face, Gladwin lowered the bugle with a military flourish, and sat down.

'Four times I sounded old Gabriel,' he said. 'By the third time those brigands were back in their saddles and by the fourth they were racing for home!' He pursed his lips. 'Happily they didn't stop to wonder what had brought

29

the cavalry this far from Fort Laramie.'

'That's the damnedest trick I've ever seen, Mr Gladwin. Guess I owe you plenty.'

Gladwin shrugged. 'You don't owe me anything.' Again the smile appeared. 'I s'pose you could always ask Miss Forrest if she has a fancy to being painted in oils.'

For several seconds Harper was silent. Was Gladwin all that he appeared to be? Then he remembered. 'You heard what Pedlar said to me?'

Gladwin nodded. 'I'm in these parts to finish a portrait of one rancher, Mr Clay Dexter. I've time to paint another before I have to be back in Cheyenne.'

He looked at Harper thoughtfully. 'You'll hurt, and you'll hurt bad, but you'll be able to move. When you've fed, get back under your bedroll. I have to be on my way, Mr Harper, or I shall lose my commission. Should I ride to Miss Forrest and explain your situation?'

Harper shook his head, and instantly regretted it. 'Thanks Mr Gladwin, but no. I'll handle this myself.'

'As you please,' Gladwin said. 'I've taken two dollars from your poke for the flour and jerky I'm leaving. There's water in the barrel that'll keep until you can get to the well,' he said. 'Your grey's out back, and your saddle and stuff are over there,' he added, pointing to a corner beyond the charcoal drawing. 'Your poke and the letter you were carrying are with your saddle.'

'Mr Gladwin, there's fifty dollars sewn into a pocket below my saddle. Take them, you've earned every dollar.'

Gladwin shook his head. 'Gabriel comes free in time of need.' He began to stand, stopped suddenly, remembering something.

'Your Winchester and gunbelt are beneath you, under the bunk.'

Harper watched while Gladwin picked up his large

carpetbag, and carried out wooden boxes, one by one, to load onto his mule, A few minutes later, mounting a moon-eyed roan that Harper could see through the open doorway, Gladwin turned away from the cabin with a shouted farewell.

Harper lay still for several minutes. Fate had played him a winning hand when Gladwin had found himself in those cottonwoods. Next time he mightn't be so lucky. But why was Pedlar so damned fired up? Why would Pedlar ride out for half a day when he must have been told that Abigail Forrest had hired someone who was already heading his way? Did that mean Pedlar hadn't wanted him even to reach Bridgetown? If the hotel clerk had heard John Meeks's death being talked about he could have told Scarred Nose who, in turn, would have told Pedlar.

Gritting his teeth against the pain, he pushed himself over the edge of the bunk to grope for his gunbelt, his hand tightening around the butt of his Peacemaker. Maybe Pedlar had been involved in John's death. If so, that gave him two reasons to kill the sonovabitch.

Harper was maybe half a mile past the high wooden arch marking the Double M ranch of Abigail Forrest when a single rider broke from a stand of cottonwoods and rode towards him. Harper reined in slowly, bringing the grey out of a lope and easing the animal to a steady walking pace. After two weeks in the Williams's cabin he was feeling a damned sight better, but the ten miles he'd ridden had found parts of his body that still needed resting.

The rider halted on the track ahead of him, maybe twenty feet away from Harper. He was a short, barrel-chested man in a rough woollen shirt, leather chaps protecting his pants. Grey hair protruded from beneath his sweat-stained hat. Instead of the lighter, work-scarred weapon of a cow-puncher, he wore at his hip a .44 Remington. A lot of iron for an old-timer on a cattle ranch, Harper reckoned.

'Howdy, stranger.'

Harper nodded a greeting but remained silent.

'You mind tellin' me your business?'

Harper looked in the direction of the cottonwoods. 'I might do that, you call your pardner over.'

The rider's expression didn't alter, and for a moment Harper wondered if he'd heard Harper's reply. Then the rider's face twisted in irritation as he turned to shout.

'Zeke! Get over here!'

From out of the stand of trees a young man appeared on a palomino, trotting his mount to halt alongside the old-timer. Despite the fine horse, Zeke wore the rough clothes and shotgun chaps of a ranch hand.

'I'm real sorry, Mr Joe,' he said, red-faced. 'I was sure I was hidden jus' like you told me.'

'You gotta lot to learn, son.'

He turned back to Harper, studying him for a few seconds. 'Guess you must be Luke Harper,' he said finally. 'Cain't be too many folks around here sportin' that many marks of a beatin'.'

He put a gnarled thumb to his chest. 'Joe Jessop's my name. I'm back givin' Miss Abigail a hand now the boys have to be away with the beeves to the railhead. This 'ere tenderfoot is Zeke. He's a lotta trouble to me. I only keep him 'round 'cos he's got a fast hoss, and can shoot that Navy on his hip a darn sight better than I ever could.'

'Aw, Mr Joe, those things you said ain't true, an' you know it,' Zeke said, but his expression showed his pleasure at Jessop's words,

Harper nudged his grey forward. Joe Jessop, he reckoned, was a darn sight smarter than he was making out.

Maybe, too, like Zeke said, he could draw that Remington as fast as he needed.

'Yeah, I'm Harper. Good to make your acquaintance, Mr Jessop. You too, Zeke. I guess you know why I'm here.'

Jessop began to turn his mount's head. 'Ride with us up to the big house,' he said.

When Harper had drawn level with the two men, Jessop turned to look directly at him. 'The Double M sure needs you, Mr Harper. Things are gettin' really bad 'round here. Soon as the boys had left, damned rustlers ran off more of our beeves. Shot poor Dan Roper in the doing of it.'

The three men rode in silence, save for when Zeke pointed out to Harper a high meadow skirted with stands of pine over to the east.

'Good lake for fishin' up there, Mr Harper, you have the time.'

'Don't be a damned fool, Zeke,' Jessop said.

After a further mile or so, the three men reached higher ground, and Harper could see the roof and the upper walls of the big house that nestled in a hollow some miles distant. The building looked substantial, built with the money, Harper assumed, that had been made over the last thirty years. Now, according to Abigail Forrest, the ranch and all it meant to her, and to the men who worked there, was under threat.

Had John Meeks ever visited the house? Harper supposed he had. In a place like Bridgetown not so many years on from the old frontier days, educated people were almost bound to meet with each other.

Over to the west, sunshine glinted on the water of a wide river. A herd of young steers, maybe no more than fifty head, pulled at the grass on the far bank. The bunch and buffalo grass was green. Abigail Forrest's cattle being driven to the railhead would need all its goodness to sustain them.

'That beef belong to Clay Dexter?' Harper asked Jessop, assuming the river marked the boundary of the Double M.

'They're ourn,' Jessop replied. 'Miss Abby owns a two-mile strip beyond the river before Mr Dexter's land. Some deal between Charlie Forrest and Walter Riley when they first arrived in these parts.'

'Could make some folks a mite ornery.'

Jessop shook his head. 'Walter Riley, God rest his soul, could water his cattle anytime he wants. When Mr Dexter bought out Walter Riley's kinfolk he got the same deal.'

None of the men spoke again until they were a couple of hundred yards from the big house. They approached from around a large corral and, as they passed a huge barn, Harper could see that his first notion of the big house was on the mark.

The walls looked as solid as an army fort, built of stone buttressed with heavy wood, and reaching maybe forty feet from ground to roof. Ten windows below the eaves set maybe six feet apart from each other ran the length of the house. At the lower level, four large windows spanned the house either side of a high doorway. Below them a deep boardwalk ran along the full length of the house. In front of the doorway, broad steps led from the edge of the boardwalk to the ground.

Twenty yards from the house, close to white-painted posts edging a small corral, stood a hitching rail. A big California sorrel, with a saddle that gleamed in the sunlight, munched at a morral. Jessop led the way, and he and Zeke waited while Harper dismounted and hitched up his grey. As he did so, footsteps sounded on the board-walk of the house.

Harper turned to see Abigail Forrest coming down the steps on the arm of a tall, slim man, a silver-grey Dakota

34

hat with its four-inch whipped brim held at his side. His dark-blue Prince Albert and shining black boots spoke of money.

Abigail Forrest's smile showed her pleasure at seeing Harper.

'I ain't seen Miss Abby look like that for a long while,' Jessop muttered before raising his voice. 'Guess you know Mr Harper, Miss Abby.' He called. 'Feller's knocked about some but he looks like what we need.'

Abigail Forrest's smile faded as if for a moment she'd remembered why she'd asked for Harper's help. Then the smile returned.

'Thank you so much for coming, Mr Harper,' she said, as the pair reached where Harper was standing. For a second she studied his bruised face, concern showing in her brown eyes.

'But I mustn't forget my manners! Clay, this is Mr Harper who I've asked for help with the cattle-thieves.' She turned to Harper. 'Mr Dexter has the ranch over the river.'

Abigail Forrest took her hand from Dexter's arm, and the two men shook hands.

'I've heard about you, Mr Harper.' Dexter said. 'You're a courageous man to keep your promise to Miss Forrest after what happened.'

Harper shrugged. 'Just stubborn, I reckon.'

Dexter nodded, as if Harper's explanation was enough. He turned to Abigail Forrest.

'I must be away, Miss Abby. Maybe in a few days we can talk again about that land on my side of the river?'

'You're always welcome at the Double M,' she said.

And that was a smart way, Harper reckoned, of avoiding an answer to Dexter's question.

He stood back to watch while Zeke dismounted to

release the feedbag from the sorrel, unhitch the horse, and hand the reins to Clay Dexter. Dexter, it appeared, was a favoured guest, no matter what business he and Miss Forrest had been discussing.

Abigail Forrest stood for a moment while Dexter rode away with a wave of his hand in her direction.

'Me an' Zeke are gonna take a look at this corral, Miss Abby,' Jessop said. 'Some work needs doin'. I can show Mr Harper the cabin, first.'

'Yes, that's good, Joe. You'll find the cabin comfortable, Mr Harper. My father had it built especially for visitors from Cheyenne. We'll meet in the house in an hour.'

'How come you know what happened to me?' Harper asked. 'You get a visit from an Englishman called Gladwin? Tall feller in a suit you can't miss.'

Abigail Forrest shook her head. 'Zeke told us. He has kinfolk the other side of the bridge who heard talk.' She frowned. 'I've heard people speaking of Mr Gladwin. Is he known to you?'

'You could say that,' Harper said. 'I reckon he saved my life.'

'Gladwin's in a lotta trouble now,' Jessop said, from astride his mount. 'You seen Jake Pedlar. Mighty proud of bein' hisself. He's holding Gladwin, threatening all sorts of danged things unless he gets his likeness painted like rich folks.'

Harper breathed in deeply. 'Miss Forrest, that meeting will have to wait,' he said. 'I got other work to do first.'

CHAPTER FOUR

The loud noise of men shouting in half-a-dozen languages and the staccato notes of a jangling pianola spilled over into Main Street, reaching Harper's ears as he turned the grey's head in front of the Golden Nugget. There were still three hours before sunset but already the saloon sounded as if business was in full swing.

Nobody had given him a second glance as he'd clattered across the wide wooden bridge that divided the settlement. South of the bridge he'd left decent folk going about their daily business. He'd seen folks in city clothes, the men tipping their hats to the ladies in their mail-order dresses. Young girls, still with their hair down, had passed him, walking with their mothers to the dry goods store. A blacksmith, surrounded by clouds of steam, had been hammering out a plate.

Ten yards over the bridge it was if he was in a different country. Hard-faced men lounged around, their eyes constantly shifting, as if looking for prey. Other men, with the appearance of miners, sat around in groups, bottles by their sides. The few women he passed looked ill and unkempt. This was Jake Pedlar's territory, and Harper was gambling that freshly shaven, and wearing a different set of trail clothes, he'd be unrecognizable to any of Pedlar's men.

He slid easily from his saddle, hitched his grey at the rail alongside half-a-dozen other horses, and stepped up to the boards. Pushing through the batwing doors into the almost stifling heat, he saw groups of men at tables that were covered in bottles and glasses. To Harper it looked as if all the nations of the world were present. Red-haired Scotsmen, heavily muscled, broad-shouldered black men, Celestials with their yellow skins, Latinos from down south, all shouting at each other, their voices almost drowning out the diamondback-rattle of shaken dice. There were women in the large room, their features showing their origins in half-a-dozen countries. Some wore skimpy shifts, some had loose cotton dresses showing bare flesh. They sat around the tables, their hands on the men's arms and shoulders. Men stood, leaning against the walls, clutching tin mugs and bottles in their hands waiting for their chance to grab a chair.

On a raised platform at the rear of the saloon, four old-timers sat, dressed in similar claw-hammer coats, squeeze boxes and fiddles at their feet, taking a break while the pianola fought a losing battle against the constant roar of loud voices and the explosions of bawdy laughter that filled the saloon. Over to Harper's left, a bar ran almost the whole length of the room. Four men in dirty white aprons bustled to and fro serving the men who shouted their orders above the noise.

Harper stepped forward. A young woman no more than seventeen years old, clad in a pink shift that fell only to her knees, took hold of his arm. The sickly pallor of her face, showing bones prominent from lack of nourishment, was made more obvious by the rouge that reddened her cheeks. As she lifted her face to look up at him the garish colour served also to emphasize the half-inch knife cut on the underside of her jaw. There was black stuff around her

38

eyes that Harper had seen before on the hurdy gurdy girls down in Texas.

'Where's Ruby?' Harper said, before the girl could speak.

The girl held onto his arm. 'In the back room,' she said. 'But she ain't a working gal. You want a gal young like me.'

'That the back room at the end of the bar?'

'Yes,' she said sulkily. 'But you're wasting your time with Ruby.'

Harper removed her hand from his arm. He put a hand in his trail pants and took out a coin. 'Here, go buy somethin' to eat.'

She snatched at the coin. 'Mister, you don't know what you're missin'.'

She turned away, to clutch at the arm of a miner, so drunk he was barely able to stand. Her smile, as she looked up into his face, didn't reach her eyes.

Harper pushed his way through the crowds of men. Halfway across the room an old man with outstretched hands begged him for a coin. Harper pushed away the man's arms, reached for a coin, and flipped the old-time fifty cents. The old man was calling for whiskey at the bar before Harper had taken two paces. Sweat was beginning to trickle down his back by the time he reached the closed door.

He knocked twice, and called out. 'Ruby Moreton!'

There was a pause, and the door opened. In front of Harper stood the biggest man Harper had seen in a long time. Maybe six and a half feet tall, the giant's huge barrel chest sported a thick red shirt decorated with a bushy black beard that fell to his midriff. Arms as thick as Harper's thighs strained against red flannel, taut over the giant's muscles. He looked down on Harper with bloodshot eyes.

'You don' come in 'ere,' he said, in an accent that Harper could barely understand. Black and broken teeth were pushed forward into Harper's face.

'Go now, cowboy!'

Harper took a step back from the man's poisonous breath. 'Tell Ruby her sister was Zeke's mother.'

'I tol' you cowboy—!'

'Let him pass, Ivan!' a woman's voice interrupted. 'An' get us a couple of drinks.'

Harper stepped into the room past the huge Ivan. The woman who'd given her orders looked up from a leather-bound ledger, pen in hand. She was small, maybe forty years old, with fair hair pushed up beneath a black comb that matched the colour of her bombazine dress.

'I'm assumin' you ain't one of these temperance people.'

'Whiskey will be fine,' Harper said. Black bombazine? First time he'd seen that worn in a saloon. The only widow-woman he remembered in a saloon was in Dodge, and she'd favoured bright green and young cowboys.

'Take the weight off. How's that smart nephew of mine?'

Harper sat down. 'Still smart, I guess. Him havin' me use those exact words about your sister.'

Ruby Moreton gave a hoarse chuckle. 'Sometimes she's my cousin, other times Zeke's my son. Depends what me and him fix up.'

She took two readymades from a box on her desk, and handed one to Harper. He fished into the pocket of his vest, and was leaning across the desk with a burning wooden match when Ivan came back with the whiskey. Without a word the giant put down the glasses and the bottle on the desk and looked at Ruby Moreton. She gave a brief nod, and he uncapped the bottle and poured two generous measures. At a further nod from the woman he turned and left the room.

She blew smoke towards the oil lamp hung above the desk.

'You here about those two gals? Helluva business. One mebbe was bad enough, two coulda ruined me.'

Harper shook his head. 'I got other business,' he said. 'But you certain both are dead? I'm told only one body's turned up.'

'You think the gals just get on the stage when they fancy? Janey went just like Bella. They'd go some place for a coupla days, come back all beaten around with more money than they'd earn here in a month. That is,' she added, 'until Bella was found outa town all cut up.'

Ruby studied him carefully. 'Anyways, how come you know Zeke?'

'I gotta job with the Double M.'

Ruby nodded as if Harper had given the answer she'd expected.

'Thought it wouldn't be too long afore that fancy lady got herself a shootist.'

She took a draw on her readymade. 'Ain't often we see another lawman this side of the bridge. I hope to hell you ain't plannin' to take over from that lame sheriff the town's got. Davis ain't likely to cause us any trouble. You don't look the type to scare easy.'

'You got the wrong idea, Ruby. I'm no lawman.'

Again Ruby let out her hoarse laugh. 'You ain't wearin' a badge you mean! You think I've lasted this long without knowing a lawman when I see one?'

Harper shrugged. 'You're gonna think what you want. Fact is, I've heard about Jake Pedlar holdin' a friend of mine. Feller's so damned salty he might get himself into more trouble he can handle.'

'The Englishman all spraddled out in his low-necked

clothes? I seen him around.' She picked loose tobacco from her upper lip. 'An' you're gonna take on that crowd of gunnies and set him free, I s'pose?'

'Somethin' like that,' Harper said. 'Zeke reckons you could tell me where they're holdin' him.'

'You're godamned lucky Jake Pedlar's down in Cheyenne. But, mister, I was wrong about you. You ain't no lawman. You're just plumb crazy!'

Harper remained silent. He drew on his readymade and took a sip of his whiskey. His expression gave away nothing. He needed Ruby maybe more than she realized. Gladwin could be held anywhere, and stumbling around looking for him this side of the bridge was the quickest way to Boot Hill.

'Don't you bring Zeke into your damned-fool notions!' Ruby snapped.

'I ain't bringin' anybody in.'

Ruby's eyes widened. 'You're gonna do it alone? You oughta be wearin' a suit like that English feller!'

Harper grinned at the notion.

'Mister, I ain't got no love for Jake Pedlar,' Ruby said. 'Sonovabitch takes a chunk of my money every month. You cause trouble for him, an' you're a friend of mine. But he's got some real tough *hombres* on his payroll. I hate to send a man to his death.'

Harper said nothing, blowing smoke above her head, and taking another sip of his whiskey. He watched the woman carefully, guessing that she was figuring the odds.

'Nobody's ever gonna know about you an' me talkin',' he said.

For almost thirty seconds Ruby's small eyes studied his face. Then she suddenly broke into a smile. 'Goddamn! I just knowed something like this was gonna happen one day! End of the street you'll find a little saloon, maybe fifty yards past where the snake-oil salesman's got his tent. Pedlar's men hang about there. That's where they're keeping your friend.'

'Thanks, Ruby.' His hand went to his vest pocket. 'Five dollars, OK?'

She shook her head. 'No charge for pals of Zeke,' she said. She looked at him carefully. 'You ain't tol' me your name, but you're Harper, I guess.'

Harper nodded, getting to his feet. A thought came to him.

'You ever come across Dr Meeks?'

'Doc Meeks? Sure! He was over here once a month, looking after my gals. He was a fine man, no preachin', just made sure the gals weren't sickenin'.' Her mouth turned down. 'Janey, she was the second gal to get herself murdered, she worshipped him. An' I reckon he was fond of her, you know, in a nice way. I'm guessin', but I reckon she used to tell him things maybe she shouldn't.' Ruby's teeth worried her lower lip.

'We're lucky we got that Doc Scott,' she said. 'But that was really sad about Doc Meeks gettin' killed.'

'You believe he got thrown from that horse?'

'That's what folks said,' Again her teeth worried her lip. 'Strange that the doc died and Janey disappeared so close to each other, them bein' such good friends, an' all.'

Harper got to his feet. 'Thanks for the help, Ruby.'

He put a finger to his hat and, starting to turn for the door, he stopped abruptly. Might as well say it, he decided.

'Young girl out there. Gotta cut on her chin.'

'Jeannie. Pretty little thing. But she don't keep company. Just gets 'em to buy drinks.'

'Kinda young even for that, ain't she?'

Ruby took a draw of her readymade, blowing smoke in Harper's direction. 'Mister, I don't own those gals. I'm in the business of selling liquor. This is a saloon. I ain't running a sewing circle.'

He gave a wry smile. 'No, I guess you ain't.'

Ten minutes later Harper reached the door of the small saloon described to him by Ruby. Unlike the Golden Nugget with its painted signboard and its batwing doors, this place was unmarked and had a solid door with an iron handle. The small window to the right of the door was smeared, and Harper was unable to see inside.

What would he find when he opened the door? Hell, the place might be empty. Only one way to find out. He checked that his Peacemaker was easy in its holster, turned the iron handle and pushed open the door.

Yellow light was thrown over the shadowy interior by oil-lamps hanging from a cross-beam below the timbered roof. The saloon was small, maybe half-a-dozen tables standing amongst the sawdust. A small, dark-haired man, a ragged towel over his arm, stood behind a barrel and plank bar over to Harper's left. Save for the four men who sat around a table over to his right there were no other customers. Harper stepped towards the bar, and a voice called out.

'Whiskey's cheaper down the street.'

Harper looked across at the men. Three of them wore rough trail clothes. One wore his pants tucked in his boots, cavalry style. Was that a knife protruding from the right boot? Harper wasn't sure. He could see that two of the players had heavy sidearms on their hips. The one who had called out, seated on the far side of the table, wearing a greasy hat, would be carrying the same.

'I've been there,' Harper said. 'Too damn noisy.'

The card-player, the only one whose face Harper could see, lifted his shoulders. 'Your money, I guess.'

Harper walked across to the bar. 'Whiskey,' he ordered.

'That'll be a dollar.'

'Feller was on the level,' Harper said.

He watched the barkeep pour out a measure, put a coin on the bar, then picked up the glass and ambled over to the table where three of the men were looking intently at their cards.

The fourth man looked up as Harper reached the table. His eyes widened, his mouth opened, and then shut like a trap. Harper was damned pleased Gladwin had brains.

He turned on his heel and went back to the bar.

'What do folks know you by?' he asked the barkeep, his voice too low to be heard by the men at the table.

'All these men call me George,' the little man said, sounding surprisingly bitter. 'My real name is Alphonse. I am from New Orleans,' he said proudly.

'OK, Alphonse,' Harper said. 'I'm gonna bet that you gotta scatter gun someplace close.'

The little man nodded slowly, his expression becoming wary.

Harper's voice remained even, just chatting to the barkeep in a friendly way if any of the three men behind him paid him any mind.

'You touch that scattergun afore I'm outa this place, an' I'm gonna kill you first.' The smile stayed on Harper's face. 'You got that?'

The barkeep's face turned ashen. 'Now, mister—'

'You got that, I said?'

'OK, mister, OK! I'm not looking for trouble.'

Harper waited a few seconds, then, sure of his man, he put down his glass. Slipping one hand into his pants pocket, he turned and went back to stand close by the table.

'Howdy, Mr Gladwin,' he said.

Gladwin looked up. He licked his lips. 'Howdy.'

The player who had warned Harper about the price of whiskey looked up at the exchange of greetings, his eyes narrowing.

'You ready to leave, Mr Gladwin?' Harper asked.

'He's stayin',' the card player said.

'I really would like to go, Mr Harper,' Gladwin said.

For an instant there was absolute stillness around the table then roars of fury erupted from the three men as they leapt to their feet.

Harper hit the nearest man between his upper lip and his nose, feeling gristle give way under the weight of the short metal bar clenched in his gloved fist. His Peacemaker, drawn with the skill of much practice, side-swiped the second player across his chin as he reached for his sidearm. Simultaneously, whiskey and broken glass showered Harper as Gladwin smashed the whiskey bottle from the table across the face of the player with the greasy hat.

Breathing heavily, Harper swung on his heel to see the barkeep stock still, his hands raised as if to ward off the menace of the Peacemaker's long barrel levelled, rock-solid, in his direction. Satisfied, Harper looked down at the three men who lay still among the sawdust, before noticing Gladwin anxiously studying his hand.

'Where the hell you learn that trick, Mr Gladwin?'

'A bar near my art school, Paris, France,' the Englishman said.

'Helluva way to learn paintin',' Harper said. 'We'd better get outa here fast. Go get your traps.'

CHAPTER FIVE

Harper, carrying a rolled sheet of pale wood-flecked paper, made his way to the Double M's big house, having left Gladwin behind in the cabin that they were now sharing. The artist had missed his appointment in Cheyenne, losing a valuable commission. When Harper had suggested he try his luck with Abigail Forrest, he'd jumped at the notion. Although when Gladwin had asked to borrow Harper's spare trail pants so he could clean his suit, Harper had wondered if it was such a good notion. Then he'd remembered Gladwin's trick with his bugle.

'Here, Mr Gladwin,' he'd said. 'Keep 'em. I was aimin' to go into town today to buy a new pair, anyways.'

He was smiling to himself as he rounded the corner of the large barn and came face to face with a pinto pony being led by a small boy dressed in bib overalls over a blue woollen shirt A battered straw hat covered most of his blond hair. His free hand held a long fish pole, its line secured to the pole with buckskin strings.

'Oh!' the boy exclaimed, as Harper disentangled himself from the pinto's head, the fish pole, and the short leading rein. 'Sorry, Mr Harper!'

'You an' your pony move like Comanches, young feller!' Harper said. He looked at the boy again. Was there something vaguely familiar about him?

'Seems you already know my John Henry. What's yourn?'

'Charles Forrest the Third,' the boy said. 'Mostly I'm called Charlie.'

'Good to meet you, Charlie. Looks a good day for fishin'.'

'I'm not s'posed to go on my own.' Charlie pulled up his nose. 'Marmee worries I'll fall in the lake, or something,' he said. 'But I'm a good swimmer, Mr Harper. I'll be safe.' He looked up at Harper. 'I'm going to bring a fish back for supper as a surprise. You promise not to tell Marmee?'

Harper grinned. 'As I haven't met your marmee, I promise.'

The boy pulled up his nose again, plainly puzzled.

'But I saw you talkin' with Marmee and Mr Dexter when Mr Joe and Zeke brought you in.'

Harper's expression didn't change. Abigail Forrest was sure proving to be a surprise. Every time he turned around she appeared as a different woman.

'Sure,' he said. 'Just slipped my mind for a second, I guess. You goin' to that lake coupla miles or so down the track?'

Charlie nodded enthusiastically.

'Then take it easy, pardner. I guess we men have to keep some things from the womenfolk.'

'Thanks, Mr Harper!'

His face shining with excitement, Charlie bounded aboard the pinto, kicked his heels into the pony's sides, and disappeared behind the barn. A fine boy, Harper thought. For a moment or two he stood still looking across the land towards the east. Maybe if his life had turned out differently, he'd have a son like Charlie. He cut the thought with a shrug of shoulders, and turned towards the big house.

A few minutes later, Harper was seated in a large room in the big house opposite Abigail Forrest. A girl had brought in coffee on a tray, and for no good reason, Harper tried to remember when he'd last drunk coffee poured into fine china from a silver pot. Sure, there was that time in the hotel when he'd taken coffee with Abigail Forrest, but the fixings weren't as fancy as the ones before him. Anyways, this was Abigail Forrest's own home, and that made it different.

'I met Charlie going for a ride,' he said. 'He looks a fine boy, rides well.'

Abigail Forrest looked at him, a flicker of amusement showing on her face. 'He needs to. One day he'll have the Double M.'

Harper hesitated. She sure was a puzzling woman. First there was that business in the alleyway, and she'd never said a word, now there's a boy around the place and no mention of his father. Maybe she'd married a Forrest. But hadn't she told him her father started the ranch thirty years ago?

He cleared his throat, put down his coffee, and picked up from the floor the roll of paper he'd brought from the cabin. Moving the tray back on the highly polished table he spread out the paper.

'Joe Jessop got a coupla your men in and I've drawn a rough map of your land as they all described it,' he explained. 'How long are your cowboys goin' to be away?'

'Thirty days,' she said. 'Twenty days to the railhead, ten back.'

Harper nodded. 'So I reckon the no-goods will try an' hurt you as soon as they can. An' now they're shootin', they ain't gonna let up.'

'They shot poor Dan Roper five days ago.'

'So I heard,' Harper said. He picked up a spoon from a

49

saucer to use as a pointer. 'My guess is they'll try again in maybe three or four days.' He tapped on the map at a position on Clay Dexter's side of the river. 'I saw about fifty head here when I rode in.'

He shifted the spoon eastwards across the map to a point high in the north-east of Double M land.

'We'll move 'em to here,' he said.

Abigail Forrest frowned. 'But we know the cattle are being run to the north. That makes it easy for the rustlers to reach them.' She pointed at lines drawn by Harper on the paper. 'They'll come onto my land through this arroyo and plan to drive the cattle back that way.'

'Yeah, that's right.' Harper put down the spoon and leaned back. 'An' in that arroyo is where we'll be waitin' for 'em!'

There was a long silence in the room. Abigail Forrest's eyes remained on the map, as if trying to conjure in her thoughts the moves by real men and real cattle intended by Harper's show with the spoon across the rough paper.

Finally, she looked up at Harper. 'There's going to be more shooting?'

'Lotta folks think shootin's too good for horse-thieves and rustlers.'

'I'm worried about my ranch hands,' she said. 'They're not gunfighters, Mr Harper.'

'They don't have to be. Enough men, and surprise will be enough. I'll need to ride across to Clay Dexter. He should lend us some men.'

Abigail Forrest shook her head. 'That will not be possible. Clay Dexter's backers in London, England, have ordered him not to get involved.'

'If nobody stops him, Pedlar's gonna start lookin' at Dexter's place.'

Again she shook her head. 'Pedlar's been told there'll

be an army of Pinkerton men on him if he touches even one calf belonging to the company in England.'

Harper knew that big companies in England had invested large amounts of money throughout the whole country since the War finished. They had what seemed like limitless funds and were ruthless in protecting their interests. They didn't make threats lightly. Pinkerton agents would cost a small fortune, but they'd pay it. No single rancher, even a successful one like Abigail Forrest, could hope to fund an operation like that. Harper tightened his lips.

'Then we're gonna have to do our best with what we've got.'

And what we've got, he thought grimly, remembering what he'd been told about the hands still around the Double M, was himself, Joe Jessop an old-timer, and the tenderfoot, Zeke.

An hour later Harper was astride his grey, holding the horse in a lope, heading for Bridgetown. Over to the east a hawk was high in the sky, wheeling around hunting for prey. Maybe he was no different from the bird. Wasn't he wheeling around trying to discover the truth about John Meeks's death?

He turned over in his mind the talk he'd had with Ruby Moreton. He'd thought it worth asking her if she'd heard anything. But even supposing she had any suspicions it was unlikely she'd say anything to a stranger. He'd been lucky that she'd given him news of Gladwin.

How significant was Ruby's mention of the deaths of both John Meek and her girl coming close to each other? Maybe there was a connection. The murdered girl, Ruby had said, used to confide in John. But what could a whore tell a respectable doctor that would lead to both their deaths?

Maybe the doctor in town could help him. What was his name again? Henry Scott, that was it. According to Abigail Forrest, Scott had arrived in Bridgetown to assist John several years ago and had stayed around when the population had grown. Like John, Scott didn't pass moral judgement. He treated patients both sides of the bridge with equal care. If there was even a hint that John's death wasn't an accident then surely Scott would have his suspicions.

Harper's thoughts returned to Abigail Forrest, and maybe, he told himself, he was thinking too much about her. She sure was a handsome woman. A puzzle, too. Everyone seemed to have a different notion of the woman she was.

The wind strengthened against his face as he swung round the last bend of the trail leading into Bridgetown. He hadn't thought so much about a woman since that time in Louisiana. Harper laughed aloud at the memory. And that hadn't turned out so good with the girl's six brothers calling him a damn yankee and promising to string him up from the nearest live oak unless he got out of town. He'd taken his leave of the tearful girl, had finished the job he'd been sent to do, and then hightailed it out of town on a mount faster than anything ridden by the southern belle's brothers.

Harper reined in his grey to a walk as the rough ground of the trail gave way to the hard-packed soil of Main Street. The bridge he'd ridden over to look for Gladwin was maybe 500 yards ahead of him, spanning the river at its most narrow point.

He walked his horse halfway towards the bridge, passing stores fronted by long boardwalks. The saloon, which allowed liquor, but no women and no gambling other than cards, opened only after noon, and its pine-planked door was closed.

Harper noted the position of the dry goods store where he planned to buy some fresh clothes including a new pair of pants. Following instructions, he turned to his right at the corner of the livery stable. Fifty yards from Main Street he halted at a hitching rail in front of a house outside of which hung a sign announcing 'Henry Scott MD', and was dismounting when the door to the house opened.

In the doorway stood a fresh-faced man in his early forties. He wore a city suit that had seen better days, a dark-blue four-in-hand over a grey shirt that showed beneath a green vest. His face showed a welcoming smile as he stepped forward the few feet between the door and a white-painted fence, and opened a small gate.

'Mr Harper, I assume. Zeke called around after he'd delivered Charlie Forrest to the schoolhouse. He told me you'd be visiting.'

'Doctor Scott,' Harper acknowledged. He undid his saddle-bag and took from it a small package, carrying it inside the house, where he laid it on a small table while he took off his gunbelt.

'On that hook will be fine,' Scott said. 'Then we'll go into my room.'

Harper hitched his gunbelt on the hook, picked up the package and followed Scott into a large room with a window overlooking the ground that ran from the house to the bank of the river. To the right of the window stood a desk behind which was a high-backed chair. Its twin stood in the middle of the room.

'I came here ten years ago to study with John Meeks,' Scott explained. His mouth twisted in a wry smile. 'Young men attend medical school now. I have to work hard to keep up.'

The sweep of his hand took in the three walls of the

room lined with books, gold-coloured titles glinting on leather covers.

'A fine library, Doctor,' Harper said.

'Bring that chair over,' Scott said. 'Many of the books belonged to my late friend Dr Meeks. When I hear from his lawyers, they'll be shipped out.' He glanced up at the shelves, regret showing in his eyes. 'I must start again alone,' he said. Scott's mouth tightened, his eyes showing his dismay at his friend's death.

'But to business, Mr Harper,' Scott continued. 'I guess you've come about Mr Roper. I've taken out the slug. There's a rib broken, but he'll be fine if the wound doesn't fester.'

'That's good to hear. I'll pass the news to Miss Abigail.'

Harper leaned forward and placed on Scott's desk the package he'd been carrying. 'This was for Doc Meeks. I guess you should have it now.'

Scott looked down at the parcel, and frowned.

'Do you know what this is?'

Harper shook his head. 'Only that it's news of some sort about doctorin'.'

Scott's eyes lit up. 'Well now, this is most interesting. I shall open it as soon as we've finished here.'

'I'm told you go across the bridge to look after Ruby Moreton's girls.'

Scott frowned slightly. 'Their lives are hard, Mr Harper, and frequently short. John always insisted that we did our best to keep them as healthy as possible. I do what I can.'

'So you knew the two murdered girls?'

'Yes, I did.' He was about to add something but Harper cut in.

'One of the girls might have said something important to John. Have you any notion what it might have been?'

'You're speaking of Janey, poor girl. I think she looked

54

upon John as some sort of older brother.' Scott shook his head. 'If she did, John said nothing to me about it.'

His frown deepened. 'I'll be frank, Mr Harper. The murder of the first girl, Bella, puzzled us both.' Scott grimaced. 'I'm not sure how to put this, but women on that side of the bridge are valued. For all the wrong reasons, of course. But Bella's death seemed so unnecessary.'

'Doc, are you sure John Meeks's death was an accident?'

Scott was obviously taken aback by the question. Then his surprised expression altered to a more thoughtful look. 'Are you some sort of lawman, Mr Harper? I know you're working for Abigail Forrest, but your questions make me wonder.'

Harper shrugged. 'I'm doin' my work for Miss Abigail. Any death 'round these parts gets my interest.'

'As far as I could tell, Mr Harper, my friend's death was a terrible accident. I'll be straight with you: I don't trust the sheriff. He spends far too much time across the bridge for the liking of decent folk. I had no reason to believe that anyone was lying, but when the sheriff and a couple of townsmen brought in John Meeks I made sure I examined his body.'

Scott sighed deeply. 'I confess, Mr Harper, we doctors have a lot to learn, but I repeat what I've said. I'm sure as I can be that John's death was an accident.'

Harper nodded. 'Thanks for talkin' with me, Doc.' He stood up from the chair as if to take his leave, but then paused and looked down at the seated doctor.

'There was somethin'. Feller from back East would like his pin back. It marks something the two of 'em did together, years back when they were studyin'. It's not valuable or anything, has the shape of a small beaver.' Harper shrugged. 'Maybe we should forget it now.'

Scott stood up. 'No, no! John's clothes are here in a trunk. I know the pin you mean.' Scott managed a smile. 'Frankly, it always puzzled me. John Meeks was a wealthy man, he dressed well with fine linen, yet he always wore the pin. It must have meant a lot to him.'

He stood up. 'Follow me, Mr Harper. This will not take a moment.'

Scott led the way out of his study, along a corridor, and opened a door of a small room. In the room were a variety of boxes, bags, a large trunk, and on a table, a pile of papers and a microscope alongside a variety of glass tubes and bottles.

Scott nodded sadly towards them. 'John and I enjoyed many evenings together,' he said. 'In the spirit of the age, Mr Harper, we hoped we might be considered men of science.'

He stepped forward to the large trunk and with some effort raised the lid. On top was a folded black Prince Albert which Scott turned back to reveal more clothes. He thrust his hand down the interior of the trunk, and pushing aside more clothing, pulled out a small leather box.

Opening it, his long fingers sorted through pins, a cigar cutter, several buttons, until he finally found the pin he'd been looking for.

He looked at the animal atop the pin. 'Yes, it is a beaver,' he said. 'I'm sure this is the one you need.'

'Thanks, Doc,' Harper said slowly, his mind only half on what Scott was saying. Instead, he was looking intently at the long green stain that marked the back of the folded Prince Albert.

'This the coat John was wearing when they brought him in?'

'I believe so. I only saw him after he'd been taken to the town's undertaker.'

'Any notion what that green stain is?'

Scott held up the coat and examined it carefully. Then he shook his head. 'It's not grass,' he said. His glance strayed to the microscope and bottles. 'I could find out given time.'

He looked up sharply. 'John never told me what was worrying him. I thought he was concerned about the fever that's broken out to the north of the territory. But now you're here, I think differently. Have you been sent here by people back East?'

Harper stretched out his hand for the pin. 'I'll be mighty grateful if you tell me what that mark is on Doc Meeks's coat,' he said.

CHAPTER SIX

The late afternoon sun had shifted to throw the mouth of the arroyo, where it met sloping ground, into shadow. Harper sat easily on a large chunk of stone, his hat pulled low on his head, a wolfskin coat wrapped around him providing protection from the falling temperature.

Three days before, the young steers from beside the river had been moved to a meadow south of the arroyo. Harper knew it wouldn't have been difficult for one of Pedlar's men to have located them. By coming from the north through the arroyo it would seem an easy job for a few men to round up the cattle and drive them off the Double M spread to the north.

Harper's mouth twisted wryly. He was beginning to wonder if maybe he'd planned this all wrong. Maybe fifty or so young steers was not a big enough prize to tempt the rustlers. If so, waiting out here for three days, running a cold camp, eating jerky and drinking cold water, was a mighty hard way of finding out.

He looked across at his companion sitting on the fallen trunk of a tree. Harper had watched him pick up his Winchester maybe a dozen times in the last few hours to check it was fully loaded. But there was no shame in that, he reckoned. Waiting to get shot at always did play hell with a man's nerves.

Gladwin's woollen hat was tied over his ears with a red bandanna, and around him was wrapped a thick woollen coat given to him by Abigail Forrest. Underneath the coat, Harper knew that Gladwin carried no sidearm. When the artist had first said that he wanted to come along, Harper had made him show what he could do with Jessop's Remington. He'd soon realized that with a sidearm Gladwin couldn't hit the side of a barn.

'I ain't takin' you up there to get you killed, Mr Gladwin,' Harper had said.

Then, begging another chance, Gladwin had marched off back to the cabin promising to return within a few minutes. To Harper's surprise, Gladwin had reappeared with one of his wooden boxes and taken from it a nigh-on brand new Winchester '73.

Later, when they'd all got over the shock of seeing Gladwin demonstrate his shooting skills, Jessop had turned to Harper. 'Damned if I know what Mr Gladwin's best at: his paintin' stuff, or firing that long gun!'

Now, waiting for the rustlers to appear, Harper knew that Gladwin could hit what he was aiming at. But killing another human being changed a man, and he'd keep Gladwin out of it if he could.

He looked across at the Englishman. 'Anyways, Mr Gladwin,' Harper said, 'how d'you come by that long gun?'

Gladwin shifted on the stump of the tree, his Winchester across his knees.

'Back East,' he said, 'I painted the wife of Mr Thomas Durant, a wealthy businessman. He was so pleased with my work, when he heard I was coming out West he gave it me on top of payment. That's how I got the commission from Clay Dexter,' he added. 'Mr Dexter happened to be with Mr Durant at the time.'

He looked down at the long gun. 'I practised with it when I got tired of eating jerky and wanted real meat.'

'I'm mighty pleased—' Harper stopped.

A long birdcall had sounded through the clear cold air.

'Riders comin',' Harper snapped. 'You know what to do!'

Gladwin was on his feet in an instant, moving fast to take up his position amid the small gathering of cottonwoods.

Harper, his own Winchester half-raised, moved quickly across the arroyo to take up a position protected by the slope of ground. He'd checked two days before that it gave him a clear firing line to the bend of the arroyo some fifty yards ahead.

The sound of hoofs clattering against the rough ground came to him. Harper raised his Winchester to his shoulder. Why only one horse? Was it one man riding ahead looking out for Double M riders? If so, that was fine. One dead rustler would serve his purpose. His finger began to squeeze the trigger as the horse's hoofs now sounded very close.

The mounted figure came around the bend. Harper felt his muscles freeze. Jesus Christ!

Abigail Forrest, holding her roan at a steady lope, was apparently unaware that she was riding towards his hidden position. Cursing beneath his breath, he stepped out, giving her enough distance to avoid startling her. She reined in and halted beside him.

Harper could still feel his hand shaking from where his finger had tightened on the long-gun's trigger. He knew his face must be white with the thought of what could have happened a few moments before.

'You goddamned little fool! I oughta pull you off that horse and tan your damned britches!'

The blood rushed to her face, then her mouth set firm. 'Don't you dare swear at me! I was only bringing you food!'

Again the air was split with a birdcall.

'Riders!' Harper snapped. He caught hold of the cheek-piece of the horse's bridle and ran the animal across towards the cottonwoods.

Gladwin stepped out from behind one of the trees.

'Get back in there,' he snapped at Gladwin.

'You ride as fast as you can east and circle back to the big house,' he ordered Abigail Forrest. He slapped the rump of the horse. 'Now get goin'!'

Harper took a moment to watch her thread her way through the trees, her head bent low to avoid the branches. His stomach still churned at the thought that he could have killed her. Then he spun on his heel, and ran across to take up his position.

Steadying his body against the near vertical slope of ground at the side of the arroyo, he raised the Winchester to his shoulder. The hoofs of the approaching horses grew louder. Three riders, maybe four, he decided, his mind now solely on the task that lay ahead.

If they turned back, Zeke and Hank Jessop were meant to cut them off from their positions on the edge of the arroyo. He didn't expect the rustlers to turn back. This way any killing would be down to him. It was the best way. After he'd left Bridgetown, Gladwin and the men of the Double M wouldn't still be remembering that they'd taken another man's life.

His muscles tensed. He breathed in deeply. As always in these situations his mind went back twenty-five years to the first time he'd gone hunting for deer. The words of the old soldier his stepfather had hired were imprinted on his brain. Easy now, squeeze the trigger, don't jerk it. His mind jumped to the present as a muffled sound reached his ears. A few seconds later, with a clatter of hoofs, three riders rounded the bend. Each man wore a bandanna covering half his face, their sidearms already raised, and held before them, as if the men were expecting trouble.

'Hold it right there!' Harper yelled.

Three slugs bit into the ground around him, the sound striking his ears a split second later. Goddamn! He pulled the trigger of the Winchester, levering to reload as the long-gun's slug struck the leading rider in the chest throwing him backwards. Again slugs thudded into the ground around him as the remaining two riders, heads now alongside the necks of their horses, charged towards him.

He had to stop them! Another ten yards closer and both riders would have him in a clear firing line. Again he fired, aiming at the rider who had swerved to his left, now maybe only twenty yards from where he stood. With a scream of pain, the rider fell back in his saddle, dragging his mount's head back, causing it to rear, the eyes of the horse wild. The hoofs of the horse briefly pawed the air, and its rider, dead already, fell backwards to the ground.

Still the other man came on, head bent low, arm extended, holding his sidearm, ready to fire when he had a clear view of Harper. Frantically Harper realized he wasn't going to make it. The mouth of the barrel of the rider's sidearm, huge, was only a few yards away. There was a shot, an animal scream, and Harper saw blood gush from the head of the rider's horse. The animal lunged sideways throwing the rustler onto the ground where he landed with a bone-crunching thud, twitched briefly, and lay still.

Harper ran forward, drawing his Peacemaker, but the man was clearly unconscious. The screams of the horse were silenced as the sound of Harper's shot bounced between the walls of the arroyo. Harper stood still, feeling the air rush out of his body, his eyes on the fallen rustler. Then he leaned against the slope, breathing in gulps of air, as Gladwin appeared from between the trees leading Harper's grey and his own mount.

'You're makin' a habit of savin' my skin, Mr Gladwin,' Harper said, his voice husky.

'I couldn't shoot him,' Gladwin said, looking at the man on the ground.

'You did fine,' Harper said, his breathing becoming normal, his muscle beginning to relax. He raised his sidearm again as the fallen rider began to stir. But the fight had gone from the fallen man, and he lay on his back staring at the sky, his eyes wide.

Harper reholstered his Peacemaker as horses sounded from around the bend of the arroyo.

'We're comin' in!' Jessop shouted.

Harper and Gladwin looked up as Jessop and Zeke rounded the bend, and rode towards them. The two men reined in beside the man on the ground.

'You seen this no-good before, Zeke?' Jessop asked.

Zeke moved his mount so he could take a good look at the man's face from which the bandanna had been pulled when he fell to the ground.

'Morgan Clements,' Zeke said. 'Really close to Jake Pedlar is what I've heard.'

Harper untied a saddle string on his grey and unhitched his coiled thirty foot of hemp.

'Go find a good tree, Joe. I'll bring along this critter.'

There was a strangled cry of terror from the man on the ground.

'Fer Chris'sakes! Please, please, don't!'

Harper looked down at him. 'Go find that tree, Joe.'

'Mr Harper!' Gladwin's voice rasped. 'What are you going to do?'

Harper looked up, his face set. 'I'm gonna hang this sonovabitch, Mr Gladwin. That's what I'm gonna do.'

'You will do no such thing!' Abigail Forrest's voice cut through the air, as she rode out of the trees towards the group of men. She reined in, her horse alongside Harper, looking down.

'I told you to go back to the big house!'

'You're not giving me orders, Mr Harper. Remember, you work for me! I saw what happened. Shooting men who attack you is legal; hanging a man in cold blood is not. This man will go to trial before a judge.'

'Horse-thieves and rustlers don't get a trial!'

'Mr Harper, if the Double M is to survive then we must live by civilized rules. This man is going to jail.'

Harper glared up at her. Her lips had set in a firm line, and her eyes returned his gaze without flinching. Even in his anger he had to admit she was a fine woman. Any woman alone in the world who could hold together a ranch the size of the Double M had the courage of ten men. But this time she was making a bad mistake.

'I hang this one, and Pedlar's gonna find it harder to send in others.'

'I understand your reasoning, Mr Harper, but we must uphold the rule of law in Bridgetown.'

'Cattle-thieves have been lynched all over the country. Nobody ever said it was against the law.'

'Those times are past. This man will face a judge.'

Harper breathed in deeply. 'That your last word?'

'Yes, Mr Harper, it is.' She held his gaze unflinching as Harper looked directly at her for a full thirty seconds.

He turned to Jessop and Zeke. 'You both OK seein' this trail trash to jail?'

They both nodded, their eyes shifting rapidly between Harper and Abigail Forrest. Jessop had the glum expression of someone who had guessed what was going to happen next.

Harper mounted his horse, sliding his Winchester into its sheath as he turned towards Abigail Forrest.

'Pedlar ain't gonna take this lyin' down,' he said. 'Next time it'll be more than just rustlin' a few head, an' wingin' a cowboy. You'd better hire another man fast. I got more important things to do.'

He touched the brim of his hat with one finger, turned his grey, and rode away without looking back.

Harper was half-lying on his bunk, his feet extended on to a chair watching Gladwin pace up and down the cabin they were planning to quit when Gladwin finished loading his mule.

Harper's bedroll was on his mount, the grey hitched to the rail outside the cabin, already fed and watered for what would be a long ride.

Halfway across the cabin, Gladwin stopped and turned to face Harper.

'Listen, Mr Harper—'

'Fer Chris'sakes, Tom, stop callin' me Mr Harper. You're makin' me feel old!'

'Mr Harper, Luke! You don't have to do this!'

'I tol' you before,' Harper said. 'It's no trouble. I ride with you towards Cheyenne until we're sure you're safe from Pedlar. Then you ride on, an' I'll come back to Bridgetown. I got unfinished business in town.'

'I don't mean that. I'm talking about—' Gladwin was cut off by a voice from outside the cabin calling his name. He turned away from Harper and went across to the door and stepped outside.

A couple of minutes later he was back. 'You'd better come outside, Luke,' he said.

Harper scrambled to his feet. ' 'Bout time I got paid for gettin' shot at.'

He stepped across the cabin and through the doorway. Now what the hell was all this about? A bunch of men and women stood a few yards from the cabin, Jessop and Zeke, a couple of the ranch hands, the cook from the main house, the girl who'd served him coffee, Abigail Forrest's maid, and two others he didn't recognize.

'What's all this about, Joe?'

Jessop cleared his throat with a nervous cough. 'Mr Harper, we un'erstand the reason why you quit. But most of us folks here have worked for Miss Abby a long time, and we think highly of her.'

There was a ripple of muttered support for Jessop's words.

'I ain't much of a man with words, Mr Harper,' Jessop continued, 'but me an' my pardners here know that Miss Abby needs you. An' that business with Clements, well, she's just tryin' to do what's right, same as always. Only maybe now she's too proud to say she wants you around. So me and my friends here, we're gonna say it for her. We'd all be mighty pleased if you'd stay.'

'And I'll second that, Luke,' Gladwin said quietly.

Harper stared at the men and women in front of him before turning around to Gladwin who looked back at him with raised eyebrows, an amused glint showing in his eyes.

Harper turned back to Jessop. 'The Double M cowboys think as much of Miss Abigail as you folks?'

'They sure do.'

A slow grin appeared on Harper's face. 'Then I guess between us all we can handle Jake Pedlar, an' anyone else who tries to bring down the Double M.'

66

As he took the couple of steps to the ground, smiles broke out on the faces of the men and women in front of him, save for Zeke who stepped alongside Jessop with a grim expression on his young face.

'Mr Harper, somethin' I gotta tell you.'

'Pedlar's men spotted you up in that arroyo,' Harper said.

Zeke's eyes widened with surprise, before he lowered his head to look down at the ground.

'Yeah,' he muttered.

'Takes courage to admit a mistake after a shootin',' Harper said. 'I admire you for it, Zeke.'

He looked in the direction of the big house and his grin broadened.

'Hope I got enough of the same when I face Miss Abby!'

CHAPTER SEVEN

Harper took the last of his coffee and put down his cup. Strange sort of world he was living in, he decided. Before he'd met Abigail Forrest he hadn't drunk coffee out of fine china with a beautiful woman since that time down south. And that was a long time ago. Maybe it was time he got back to Boston.

'You're not angry with Zeke?' Abigail Forrest asked.

'Zeke's fine,' he said.

'He tried to warn me as I rode towards you,' she said. 'I guess those men saw him.'

She bit her lip. 'I'm sorry I was so foolish.' Then she looked at him directly. 'But I'm glad I was there.'

'The sheriff gonna hold that nogood Clements?'

'I don't trust Sheriff Davis, but he'll not risk the anger of the town council, and Miss Esther Morris will be in Bridgetown next month.'

Before Harper had chance to ask how a Miss Esther Morris could fit with his question there was a knock at the door.

Abigail Forrest stood up with a swirl of her blue cotton dress, and Harper caught a glimpse of expensive buttoned shoes as she crossed the room to the door. She sure was a fancy dresser for a rancher. He overheard a brief exchange of words between the two women, and Abigail Forrest returned to her chair.

'Clay Dexter is about to call on me,' she said.

The thought crossed Harper's mind that she'd dressed in fancy clothes for Dexter's call. On his feet since Abigail Forrest had stood, he picked up his hat from a side table.

'I'll be on my way. We'll talk later.'

'No, please wait. I'd like you to be here.'

'Maybe he'll want to talk about that land of yourn.'

'Yes,' she said. 'Clay can be very persuasive.'

'And you don't want to sell?'

As she shook her head, the door opened.

'Mr Dexter, ma'am,' said a girl in a piping tone.

Dexter stepped into the room. Unlike his previous visit, he wore trail clothes, his pants pushed into expensive tooled boots. On top of his woollen shirt he wore a fine leather trail jacket.

'Good day to you, Miss Abby. I hope you'll forgive the unexpected call.'

'You're always welcome, Clay. You know that.'

'Good to see you again, Mr Harper,' Dexter said, and hesitated fractionally, before turning back to Abigail Forrest.

'I called in on my way to town. I wanted to talk business, but I can return later if you wish.'

'That will not be necessary. I've asked Mr Harper to stay.'

Dexter frowned, obviously surprised by her response. But if she was aware of Dexter's reaction, she ignored it.

'Shall we all sit down?' she said, gesturing to the chairs.

She led the way across the large room, Dexter glancing at the coffee pot and cups on the small table. When Abigail Forrest was settled, her long skirts arranged, both men took their seats.

Again Dexter glanced at Harper, as if uncertain about

his presence, before he addressed Abigail Forrest.

'You must acknowledge, Miss Abby, the present situation makes little sense. My partners in England are more than happy to pay well above the market price for the strip of land on my side of the river. Indeed, they're as puzzled as I am how such an arrangement was ever made.'

'The Shoshone considered parts of it as holy. My father swore an oath that he would protect it when the Shoshone were no longer here.'

Dexter nodded slowly. 'But the world moves on,' he said. 'And if ownership of the Double M changed, I could lose my water rights,'

'Then help Miss Abby to handle Jake Pedlar, and ownership will not change,' Harper said.

Dexter's expression hardened. Without turning in Harper's direction he snapped out his words. 'I understand you're fast with a gun, Mr Harper, that doesn't mean you're fast to understand land law.'

Harper was silent for a moment. 'Guess I had to be fast sittin' round a table with Thomas Durant,' he said finally.

Dexter was suddenly still, his jaw dropping slightly, his eyes wide open as he jerked his head around to stare at Harper.

'What did you say—?'

He broke off abruptly, and stood up from his chair. 'We'll talk later, Miss Abby. This was maybe a poor time to discuss such an issue after your troubles yesterday. Forgive me, but I'm already late for an appointment in town. I must bid you good day.'

He gave a half bow in the direction of Abigail Forrest and nodded curtly to Harper. Without waiting for a response from either, he turned on his heel and left the room without a further word. There was silence in the room for several seconds. Harper picked up his hat from the table where he'd replaced it on Dexter's arrival.

'I sure struck gold there, Miss Abby,' he said.

Without replying, Abigail Forrest walked over to a credenza. With her back to Harper, she opened a drawer, took out something and came back to where Harper was standing.

'I think this belongs to you,' she said. 'I've been meaning to return it.'

Harper waited, expecting her to mention the incident near the livery stable in Plainsville. When he realized that she was going to add nothing further, he nodded.

'Looks like the bandanna I lost somewhere. Thanks,' he said.

Unspoken words hung in the air for several moments until Abigail Forrest broke the silence.

'That name you mentioned, Thomas Durant,' she said, as if nothing had passed between them. 'Who is he?'

'He's a businessman of some sort back East. That's as much as I know,' Harper said. 'I was running a bluff. Tom Gladwin mentioned his name.' He grinned. 'Guess I won the pot.'

A light danced in her brown eyes. 'I guess you did, Mr Harper.'

For fully thirty seconds he looked down at her, her blonde hair level and close with his shoulder, neither of them moving.

'You gonna let Tom Gladwin paint your portrait?' Harper asked finally.

'Mr Harper! Mr Harper, sir!'

Harper had just left the big house and was walking towards the cabin when he heard his name being called. A buggy stood by the corral where Zeke and Joe Jessop were working on renewing posts. From it stepped down the lean figure of Henry Scott. The skirts of the yellow slicker covering his city suit flapped in the wind as he hurried towards Harper.

'Doc Scott! What brings you to the Double M?'

'Mr Harper, I drove straight over,' Henry Scott said. 'I really don't know what to do next!' He held out his hand. 'Two hours ago I found this in John's desk.'

Harper took the small brooch from Scott. It was a cheap imitation of an Italian cameo, a woman's head in white on a plum-coloured base edged with gold-coloured wire. Half of the woman's face was covered in a brown stain.

Harper frowned. 'I ain't followin' you, Doc. What's so important about this?'

Scott breathed in deeply. 'I've seen it before,' he said. 'You remember the first girl to be murdered, the one called Bella? This brooch was hers, I'm sure. I must have seen it a dozen times at the Nugget. She wore it all the time.'

'The brown stain?'

'Human blood,' Scott said. He sucked in his cheeks before blowing out his breath, his face taut. He turned away from Harper, as if not wanting to meet his eyes. 'This morning I remembered the secret drawer in John's desk. The brooch was there wrapped in cloth.'

'I heard her body was found on the trail outa town. Did Doc Meeks examine her?'

Scott shook his head, his eyes clouding. 'He'd gone to Cheyenne the day before. I examined Bella's body.'

Harper dropped the brooch into the pocket of his trail coat. 'We'll keep this between us, Doc. It's too soon for folks to be thinkin' about reasons, an' comin' up with all the wrong ones.'

Scott nodded vigorously. 'John was a fine man, Mr

Harper, there must be an innocent explanation.'

He took from his waistcoat pocket a large watch. 'Now I must get back to town. I've patients waiting. Oh yes,' he added, 'I'm still working on that plant stain.'

Harper watched him walk back to his buggy, unhitch his horse, its belly large with too much feed, and turn away with a wave to Harper, and shouted farewells to Zeke and Frank Jessop.

'What did Doctor Scott want?'

Harper turned to see Abigail Forrest a few yards behind him.

'Some business about John Meeks,' he said. He looked at her thoughtfully. 'Do you know exactly where his body was found?'

'At a place called Pioneers' Camp.' She smiled. 'Pioneers haven't camped there for ten years but we still use the name.'

'You fancy a buggy ride?'

She looked up at the sky. 'I'll change into something practical. Ask Zeke to get the buggy hitched up.'

Harper stood for a few moments, watching her walk back to the big house, before he went across to the corral.

'Zeke! Miss Abby needs the buggy. We're goin' for a ride.'

A big smile showed on the face of the young man as he leaned his axe against one of the posts.

'Sure thing, Mr Harper! I reckon the day's just fine seein' you an'—'

'Shut your damned mouth, and get the buggy out!' Joe Jessop said, an expression of resignation on his face. 'When Mr Harper wants to hear what you're reckonin' he'll damn well ask.'

'This is Pioneers' Camp,' said Abigail Forrest.

Harper reined in the buggy horse, and sat still, looking around him. The ground on both sides of the trail was covered in bunch and buffalo grass with maybe an occasional bunch of wild daisies. High, and to his right, several hundred yards away, stood a stand of trees on a ridge which stretched to the north.

To his left, the ground fell away in a gradual slope until it reached an open meadow of several acres edged on the west side by the river.

Abigail Forrest pointed at a stack of old blackened stones standing no more than twenty feet from where Harper had halted the buggy. Harper guessed the stones had been used in the past to surround a fire. The pioneers would have camped close to what was now a regular trail, using the high ridge as protection from the weather while having water close at hand.

'John Meeks was found dead, his body against the stones.'

'How come you're so sure?' Harper said.

Her eyes widened. 'I thought you knew. There were three of us returning from Clay Dexter's, the Reverend Martin and his wife and myself. The reverend took the buggy into town while Mrs Martin and I stayed with the doctor.'

'How about John's horse?'

'A big roan. It had strayed about a quarter of a mile. One of the townsmen found it, and took it to the town's livery.'

Harper nodded. 'I'm gonna take a look down at those stones. You wanna stay here?'

She shook her head. 'I'll walk down with you. Esther Morris will want every detail. I need to refresh my memory.'

Harper frowned. 'You mind tellin' me who this Esther

Morris is? That's the second time you've named her.'

'Esther Morris comes from South Pass. She's the territory's first woman Justice of the Peace. Maybe she's the first woman in the country to hold the position.'

Harper remembered then what Sheriff Bolden had said that time Abigail Forrest had entered the sheriff's office. About her knowing more about the law than Bolden ever would.

Harper remembered the piles of books that had stood around the room where he'd sat with Abby, as he now thought of her, and Clay Dexter.

'An' you're aimin' to be the second, I guess!'

He jumped out of the buggy and held out his hand for Abby to step down.

They walked the twenty feet or so to the stones, and Harper squatted to inspect the brown stains on the jagged edge of the large stone. He'd seen similar brown stains that morning on the brooch which nestled inside the pocket of his trail coat.

'His head was hard against that stone,' she said. 'His horse must have thrown him. Maybe spooked; we can only guess.'

'I reckon you're—' He broke off suddenly, his head jerking up to leave him staring to the north.

He reached out, grabbing her by the arm.

'Fast!' he ordered. 'Back to the buggy!'

'What's wrong?' She gasped, as she was half pulled in the direction of the buggy.

'Why are you doing that?' She gasped again, as she saw Harper draw his Peacemaker, as they both clambered into the buggy. His Peacemaker held at the ready, the reins in his left hand, he urged the buggy horse forward.

'Riders,' he snapped. 'Lots of 'em!'

The buggy horse broke into a strong trot, but Harper

knew they didn't stand a chance. The buggy had barely gone fifty yards before the smack of horses' hoofs against the dirt of the trail reached their ears and around a bend rode into sight a dozen men, led by a dark-skinned man with angular features, a fancy leather vest over his work shirt, and silver slathered on his spurs. Twenty yards from the buggy the riders fanned out to line up across the trail.

There was a sharp intake of breath from Abigail Forrest.

'Jake Pedlar!'

'You shoot that cannon, Harper, an' that fine lady's dead!' Pedlar shouted. He stood up in his stirrups. 'I got two sharpshooters here, kill her stone dead in a second. So you put that goddamn sidearm away right now!'

'Take it easy, Pedlar. No sense in getting riled,' Harper called. He eased his Peacemaker into its holster.

'Take the reins,' he said softly, and handed them to her.

'You beat three of my men, Harper, in my own place. I cain't be doin' with that,' Pedlar shouted. 'This is between you an' me. An' fancy tricks with a bugle ain't gonna save you this time.'

'Tell you what I'm gonna do, Pedlar,' Harper called. 'I'm gonna step down and walk ten yards. You let Miss Forrest drive her buggy away, an' we'll settle it here. Just you an' me if you got the stomach for it.'

Abigail Forrest let out a cry of protest. 'I'm staying right here! Jake Pedlar, the law will catch up with you and your murdering ways. I'll not leave so you can commit another!'

Pedlar eased back into his saddle. 'You're a fine lady, like I said, Miss Forrest. But that gunslinger's working for you. You take that buggy outa here, or maybe you're gonna find out what you been missin' since that no-good husband of yourn quit town!'

'How dare you!'

76

Abigail Forrest cracked the reins over the horse's head, setting the buggy charging towards the line of men. She'd barely moved ten feet when there was the crack of Winchester fire. Caught unawares for a moment by her actions, Harper snatched at the reins, hauling back on the horse's head.

What the hell was going on? An icy hand clutched at his heart. Had she been shot?

Ahead of him, Pedlar's horse was skittering to the side, as were some of the horses either side of him. Then a shout came from the stand of trees high to their right.

'Hold it, Pedlar! Or you're a dead man!'

Again there was the crack of rifle fire and dirt spurted five yards ahead of Pedlar and his men.

Who the hell was up there? Was it Tom?

Pedlar, his mount under control once more, barked out three words.

'Get that sonovabitch!'

Without further prompting, two riders on the flank broke away, rifles held high, and charged towards the ridge. Fifty yards up the slope they began to fire at random, peppering the branches with slapping sounds clear to Harper.

There was a pause, the men covering the remaining fifty yards to the trees, their heads low down. There was the crack of a rifle, then another. Within seconds of each other both men were swept from their saddles, their lifeless bodies crashing to the ground.

'Turn around, Pedlar! Take your men out of here. And I'll be watching all the way!'

'Who's up there?' Abigail Forrest's voice was husky with tension.

Harper didn't answer, looking ahead at the line of men as he saw, rather than heard, Pedlar give an order. The riders began to turn, and with a shout of fury from Pedlar, as he took the lead, they broke into a gallop.

As Harper watched, his hand resting on the butt of his sidearm, Pedlar and his men rode out of sight around the bend in the trail, the drumming of their horses' hoofs slowly fading.

Harper looked up towards the trees. A rider, his head bent low over his horse to avoid overhanging branches, started down the slope. He and Abigail Forrest sat unmoving in the buggy as the rider reached them.

The rider put a finger to the brim of his Dakota in the direction of Abigail Forrest.

'I'm sure glad I was out riding,' Clay Dexter said.

CHAPTER EIGHT

The buggy rolled off the rough ground of the trail and hit the hardpack of Main Street in Bridgetown. Clay Dexter, riding alongside the buggy, pointed at the sheriff's office.

'Davis finally showed his true colours. Lit out of town last night, so I've been told,' he said.

'So who's wearing the badge?' Harper asked.

'Nobody, unless you count the old feller who was deputy.'

'But that's nonsense!' Abigail Forrest exclaimed. 'Fred Wilkins only did odd jobs around the town. He was never a real deputy.'

'That no-good Morgan Clements still in the cage?' Harper asked.

'I guess so. The town'll need a sheriff mighty fast.' Dexter reined in, as his mount and the buggy reached the path to the doctor's house.

Harper drew the buggy to a halt and his fingers brushed those of Abby as he handed across the reins. Save for a faint pallor about her cheeks there was little sign that scarcely an hour before she'd been threatened by Pedlar and his gang of trail-trash.

At the first rifle shot, when she whipped the buggy forward, he thought she'd been hit. He'd have died at Pioneers' Camp alongside her, for he knew that with her dead he'd have killed as many of Pedlar's men as he could, before he himself was gunned down.

'Mr Dexter will ride with you back to the Double M,' he said.

'One of Joe Jessop's horses is in the livery,' Abby said. 'You can ride it home.'

Harper stood down to the hardpack, and looked up at Dexter. 'I'm obliged to you, Mr Dexter.'

With a final touch of his finger to his hat, he stood watching the buggy drive away, Dexter's mount trotting alongside. Goddamn! An hour ago he was heading for a gunfight, now he was standing around like some lost day-old calf looking for its supper. Abby was a fine woman, and he wasn't going to dwell too much about what he'd heard from Jake Pedlar.

He spun on his heel and walked the twenty yards to the doctor's house. As he reached the picket fence a young woman carrying a baby wrapped in a woollen shawl appeared at the open door of the house, Scott a pace or two behind her.

'The babe will be fine,' Harper heard the doctor say.

Harper stood back as the woman hurried past him, a mixed expression of relief and delight on her face.

'Come in, Mr Harper. I've news for you.'

Harper unbuckled his gunbelt, placing it on a convenient chair as he entered the house, and followed the doctor through to his study. On the desk a large book lay open, showing a variety of plants and grasses, all carefully drawn and coloured by hand.

'This was John's own work,' Scott said, bending over the book. 'We divided our studies. John studied the plants of the territory, and I concentrated on animals. That's why it's taken so long for me to find your answer.'

Scott placed a finger on one illustration. 'The green

stain on John's Prince Albert is from the Monument plant. It's not all that common around these parts, most are found further to the north. The Shoshone use it for medicine.'

Harper bent to look at the illustration. He guessed that great care had gone into the use of the water-colours which decorated the stiff paper. A plant, roughly the shape of a miniature pine, it's thick stalk thrusting up from the ground to meet rough green leaves, occupied most of the left hand page.

'Doc, you talked about the fever up north. Did John go up there to take look? Could he have stained his coat on a visit?'

Scott shook his head. 'We got our news of the fever by letters brought by the stage. We were too busy here. Lots of the babies in town were ill.'

'But you're sure the stain's from a Monument plant?'

'Absolutely.'

Harper stood up, a frown on his face. 'Thanks for your work, Doc. How much do I owe you?'

Scott shook his head. 'There's no charge,' he said, and sighed heavily. 'I only wish I could report the same success with that Double M boy, Roper. The wound's started to fester, and I'm worried.'

'Same as in the War, I guess. Mostly a matter of luck,' Harper said.

He had a memory flash of the hospital tents after Gettysburg, the surgeons in their bloodstained aprons, frustration showing in their eyes, as yet another man died of his wounds.

His eyes fell to the illustration again. 'You any notion where I might find this Monument plant? John must have found one not too far distant.'

Scott shook his head. 'No, but the Shoshone at Smith's

livery could maybe help you.' He smiled. 'If your Shoshone's not up to much, Smith can help.'

Five minutes after trying to talk with the Shoshone at the livery, Harper was damned glad Smith returned from looking at a horse he was thinking of buying. The few words Harper had picked up from Comanche prisoners, and from the Apache guides who'd been attached to his own troop, seemed to leave the Shoshone as baffled as much as Harper's English. Finally Harper gave up, and Smith, the livery owner, stepped forward to offer his services as an interpreter.

'For a dollar, of course, Mr Harper,' he said, rubbing his hands at what he appeared to consider an unexpected windfall. 'Folks have to make a livin' anyways they can, afore that Pedlar feller takes over this town.'

Resolving never to bring his horse to Smith's livery, Harper gave him a couple of coins, and explained what he wanted. By the expression of the Shoshone's face the Indian grasped immediately what was being asked of him. He took Harper by the arm and led him out into Main Street, Smith following on.

'Just have him point in the direction and give me some notion of the distance,' Harper ordered Smith.

'Sure, I can do that,' Smith said, immediately barking a few words at the Shoshone who stood waiting, his dark eyes intent on Smith's face. At Smith's words the Shoshone nodded vigorously, and held his two hands tightly against his stomach. An aching belly, he seemed to be saying. Then he turned, pointed to the north, and said something to Smith.

'At our distances, he reckons ten or fifteen miles,' Smith said. 'Maybe half a day's ride. I can sell you a good horse for that, if you want.'

'I gotta good horse,' Harper said. His looked doubtfully at the Shoshone. 'He's sure he's got the right direction?'

There was a rapid exchange of words between Smith and the Shoshone.

'He's sure,' Smith said. 'He said it's the only place 'round these parts.'

'You've earned your dollar,' Harper said, and walked away in the direction of the saloon. He hadn't got the answer from the Shoshone he was expecting. He needed to think, and a whiskey would help. There was something going on here he hadn't got a handle on.

Fifty yards along Main Street Harper pushed through the doors of the Paradise. Inside, the place smelled clean as if it had only opened a short time before. He stood at the entrance allowing his eyes to adjust to the shadows after the bright light outside. He saw the saloon was no different to the hundreds he'd been in before, sawdust on the floor, a bar over to his left running the length of the room, an open space with tables and chairs and a pot-bellied stove standing in a corner surrounded by a few high-backed chairs. All the fixings, even the neatly dressed little fat man behind the bar, showed it was not a saloon where cowboys got stinking drunk and started trouble. If you want that, the fixings said, go over the other side of the bridge.

So, as he moved to the bar, Harper was surprised to see the three men playing cards in the corner over to his right, bottles and money on the table in front of them. Their mean faces, their hard eyes as they looked up from their cards, the heavy iron on their hips, all were wrong for the Paradise. And the uneasy expression on the barkeep's face, as he shot nervous looks at the men, showed he was used to different custom.

Smith's words about Pedlar taking over the town came

to Harper's mind. Was the presence of the three men one of the first signs that Sheriff Davis had left town? Were they checking out this side of the bridge for Pedlar? What the hell! He was beginning to think like a pilgrim from back East. He was here for a couple of drinks, nothing more. Three men playing cards in a saloon were no concern of his.

'Whiskey,' he said, reaching the bar.

'Fifty cents, mister.'

The little man filled the shot glass, and put down the bottle on the counter. 'More there if you want it.' Again, his eyes flickered in the direction of the three men in the corner.

Harper downed the whiskey in one gulp and poured himself a second shot. The spirit warmed his insides pleasantly. The taste was different from that he was used to back East, but it sure wasn't the busthead liquor he'd been drinking along the trail.

He breathed in deeply, feeling for the muslin bag of Bull Durham beneath his vest. He took out a paper and rolled a smoke, lighting it with a wooden match. The sharp smoke caught at his throat before hitting his lungs. He breathed in deeply. It had sure been a hell of a day. When he'd rolled out of his bunk that morning he was expecting to be riding towards Cheyenne. He'd spent time grooming his grey for what he'd expected was going to be a long ride. Then everything changed.

Sure, he'd have returned to Bridgetown, after seeing Tom Gladwin safely away. With or without Abby he'd have still returned to ride out to Pioneers' Camp, and to spend time with Doc Scott. He'd not rest until he found out what really happened to John Meeks. He was becoming more convinced each day that John's death was no accident. But what was the reason for his murder? If only his letter had given even a hint of what was happening in Bridgetown.

A couple of questions nagged at him. When he'd been sitting in the buggy before Pedlar had arrived, he'd taken a good look around Pioneers' Camp. There were no Monument plants out there, he was sure, only bunch and buffalo grass and the few wild daisies he'd recognized. If Monument plants had been around there the Shoshone at the livery would have known about them.

The Indian wouldn't have made a mistake. Once he'd understood from Smith what was needed he hadn't hesitated. But when they'd gone into Main Street he'd been pointing in the direction of Clay Dexter's spread, and not, as Harper expected, beyond Jake Pedlar's territory.

The shadows in the corner of Harper's vision shifted and he glanced up to see a tall, black man, a trail jacket covering an old blue army shirt, push through the doorway and walk up to the bar. He carried a saddle-bag, and his gait was that of a proud man, his shoulders back, his head held high.

'I ain't slept in a bed for over a month,' the man said to the barkeep, weariness showing in his voice. 'An' I'm sure lookin' forward to a whiskey!'

'Comin' up, stranger,' the barkeep said, reaching for a shot glass.

'Hold it, Shorty!'

Harper glanced up at the mirror behind the bar to see the three men staring hard at the man. The one in the middle, on the other side of the table, wearing a dark red mackinaw, must have been the one who had spoken.

'You hear me, Shorty? I ain't drinkin' in the same place as some damned buffalo soldier.' Mackinaw pointed a grubby forefinger at the black man. 'You!' he said. 'You wanna whiskey, get over to the Nugget, other side o' the bridge. They ain't so fussy over there.'

The ex-soldier stood, his back to the bar, looking at the three men for a few seconds, his arms loose by his sides, his fists opening and closing. Then slowly and deliberately he turned his back on the men. Harper, keeping the men in view, saw them exchange glances with each other, before their eyes shifted again to their cards.

'You gonna sell me a drink?'

The little man's eyes flickered in the direction of the men at the table.

'I'm truly sorry, but I can't,' the little man spluttered. Then he stood up straighter, as if summoning up his better self. 'Another time, maybe.'

'Thanks, mister,' the man said resignedly. 'Sure, some other time. Guess I'll ride over the bridge.'

He picked up the saddle-bag which he'd placed at his feet when he'd moved up to the bar, and stepped away.

'Hey, soldier! What do folks know you by?'

The man turned towards Harper in response to the question.

'Name's Sam Monroe, mister.' He lifted his massive shoulders. 'Ain't lookin' fer trouble. Jes' lookin' fer work.'

Harper slid his bottle four feet along the bar. 'Here, Sam. Let me buy you a drink.' He looked at the barkeep. 'Give him a glass, Shorty.'

The little man's eyes flickered again in the direction of the card players. He opened his mouth to protest, and then saw the set of Harper's mouth. Quickly, he scrabbled below the bar and produced a shot glass.

'Stranger!'

Harper looked across to the cardplayers. Mackinaw had put his cards face down on the table and was glaring across the saloon in Harper's direction.

'You talkin' to me?' Harper said.

'I guess you don't hear so good, stranger. It ain't my

custom to drink with buffalo soldiers.'

Harper shrugged. 'This feller's drinkin' with me. If you don't like that, then you got an argument with me, not him.'

Mackinaw said something under his breath to the other two men. They put down their cards, shifting their chairs away from the table. Harper put down his glass on the bar.

'I'll go some other place,' said Monroe.

'Sure,' said Harper, not taking his eyes off the three men. 'But have your drink first.'

The slug, fired from a derringer held below the card table as Mackinaw shifted in his chair, flicked at the sleeve of Harper's trail jacket and buried itself into the bar. The crack of the little weapon matched splinters flying in the air.

Before any of the three men could make a further move, Harper's Peacemaker slid smoothly from leather to be held at arm's length pointing at Mackinaw's heart.

'You've had your shot,' he said evenly. 'I guess it's my turn now.'

From behind the bar came a strangled gasp from the little man.

Harper swung his sidearm in a short curve before bringing it back to line up on Mackinaw. 'As you're in this together, maybe I should make it three.'

The metallic click of the Peacemaker sounded as it was cocked.

'Fer Chris'sakes, mister,' said one, his voice breaking.

'There's no sheriff hereabouts,' Harper said. 'I got two witnesses to say you fired first.'

'You don't have to do this, mister,' said Monroe. 'It ain't the first time I run into this sorta trouble. You don' have to kill a man over a whiskey.'

The three men, faces ashen with fear, sat as if made

from stone, their eyes fixed on the barrel of Harper's Peacemaker. For several seconds nobody moved. Finally, as if he'd thought through a problem and come up with a satisfactory answer, Harper nodded. His Peacemaker still held at arm's length, he eased the hammer.

'Pick up your whiskey, all three of you trail trash,' Harper ordered. 'An' get over here.'

Puzzled frowns appeared on all three faces.

'Huh?'

'I said pick up your whiskey, an' bring 'em over here. Shorty! Pour Sam a drink.'

'Right away, sir! Glad to!' the little man said hastily.

Harper watched the three men grab at their money before picking up their glasses, their eyes flicking between each other before coming back to Harper. He knew if they tried to rush him he'd be forced to shoot. But the heads of all three were down, their eyes on the floor of the saloon. Sure now that the fight had gone from them, he lowered his Peacemaker to his side.

When the men were a few feet from him, he gestured with his sidearm.

'Everyone drinks,' he ordered.

He watched as the three downed their whiskey, one with trembling fingers, gagging as he gulped, drops of the spirit running down his chin. Mackinaw's face, despite having turned ashen, was now covered in rivulets of sweat. From Monroe there came a contented sigh, and then the gurgling of the bottle as the barkeep poured him another drink.

'On the house, Mr Monroe,' Shorty said.

Harper raised his Peacemaker again to hold it on the three.

'Now put five dollars on the bar. You ruined my trail jacket, an' you gotta pay.'

Expressionless, he waited while the three men frantically sorted through coins and placed sufficient money on the bar.

'Now get outa here, across the bridge, afore I change my mind.'

Harper watched as the three men made a hasty exit from the saloon, mounting their horses without saying a word to each other, and riding out of sight towards the bridge.

Harper slid his sidearm back into its holster. The atmosphere in the saloon, until then as taut as a Comanche bowstring, began to ease.

Shorty expelled breath with a loud sigh of relief. The little barkeeper gave a brief chuckle. 'You was bluffin' there, Mr Harper. You know, playin' a poker hand? Jest throwin' a fright into 'em, I guess!'

His smile faded as Harper turned towards him, his eyes hard. Then the smile reappeared as Harper visibly relaxed.

'I'll take another drink, Shorty.' He turned to Monroe. 'Ride out to the Double M,' Harper said. 'There's work goin' there. Tell 'em Luke Harper sent you.'

His eyes shifted to the doorway, his muscles tensing, his hand dropping to his Peacemaker, as the light from the doorway was blotted out by three figures.

'We got bad news, Mr Harper!' Zeke said, two paces ahead of Joe Jessop and Tom Gladwin. 'This town's gonna need you!'

CHAPTER NINE

Harper was leaning against the top rail of the small corral watching Charlie ride his pinto around within the picket posts. The boy had a frown of concentration on his face, the reins in one hand, the other resting easily by his leg. Save for the black tooled boots he always wore, he was dressed in pants and a shirt which had both seen better days. Unusually for Charlie he was bareheaded, and there was a long smudge of dirt on one side of his face.

'You up for one last time, Charlie?' Harper called.

A cry of delight came from the boy. 'Sure am, Mr Harper!'

'If you're hurtin', we can try another day. I ain't gonna think less o' you.'

'I'm fine! Let's try once more. Marmee'll be out soon!'

'OK, when I give the signal! But first you slow old Dollar down, or you're gonna break your neck!'

Obediently, Charlie reined in, bringing Dollar out of his lope to take up a brisk trot. Harper waited until both animal and boy had settled. Satisfied, he pursed his lips and blew a piercing whistle.

Instantly, Charlie kicked his feet from his irons, threw himself forward to the horse's neck as his leg came over the saddle, and rolled from the pinto, hitting the ground to roll over and over. In an instant he'd leapt to his feet, his breath coming in short bursts.

'I did it, Mr Harper!' he finally managed to shout, his hands above his head in a gesture of triumph. 'Just like you did when that Mexican bandit shot your horse!'

'And if his mama sees that,' said a soft voice behind Harper, 'She'll probably cut off your *cojones*!'

Harper swung around, grinned when he saw Tom Gladwin, and turned back to look across the corral.

'Fine, Charlie!' Harper called. 'Go get yourself and Dollar cleaned up. Maybe you'd better make it quick!'

'Yes, Mr Harper!'

Charlie ran across the corral to his pony which stood in the middle of the corral, reins falling to the ground. Harper could see the big grin on the boy's face as Charlie marched in the direction of the barn. He broke into an excited chatter when he reached Sam Monroe, as the ex-soldier opened the gate leading out of the corral.

Harper said over his shoulder. 'Charlie asked me if he could shoot my Peacemaker. I reckoned this was safer.'

He raised a hand as the boy, turning back in Harper's direction, gave another triumphant wave. Harper continued to look across the corral until Charlie and Sam entered the barn.

'How's the paintin' goin'?' Harper asked without turning.

'It's not easy. She's not an attractive woman.'

Harper's head jerked around. 'What the hell d'you mean?'

He stopped suddenly, seeing the expression on Gladwin's face. Hell! He felt like some tenderfoot at his first poker table. His thoughts must be plastered across his face. Gladwin's face was wreathed with a wide smile, his eyes dancing with humour.

'What's that I've heard you say? Sure struck gold there, Luke!'

Harper lifted his shoulders. 'Yeah, guess you did.'

He became aware that Gladwin was studying him carefully.

'Is this business about Davis troubling you, Luke? I'm not surprised the council's offered you the badge.'

Harper shook his head. 'I gotta think more about that,' he said. 'But there's somethin' else.'

He described to Gladwin how Dr Scott had identified the green stain on John Meeks's coat, and where the Shoshone had told him that Monument plants could be found.

'I rode out to Dexter's place,' Harper said. 'Took a good look 'round. The plants were there, okay. A few of 'em crushed.' He reached in his vest pocket. 'I also found this.'

Gladwin looked down at Harper's outstretched hand.

'A button?'

'From John Meeks's Prince Albert. I saw his coat at Doc Scott's place.'

The Englishman's eyes gleamed. 'You think the doctor was killed out there, and his body shifted?'

Harper nodded slowly. 'I reckon that's what did happen,' he said. 'An' there's more. I saw Jake Pedlar ride alone across Dexter's land and go into the big house. Just as if he'd done that lotsa times. I'm thinkin' Dexter and Pedlar could be in cahoots on this rustlin' business.'

Gladwin shook his head. 'That makes no sense, Luke. You said yourself if it hadn't been Dexter there out at Pioneers' Camp you and Miss Abby could have both been killed.'

Harper nodded slowly. 'Yeah, that's what's puzzlin' me. Reckon I'm gonna have to think about it some more.'

'Have you decided what to do about wearing the badge? The town needs you, Luke. The town council, Miss Abby, the reverend, they all want you as sheriff.'

'Zeke's sure about what he's heard?'

Gladwin nodded. 'He's been told by some woman friend of his across the bridge. Pedlar's aiming to break Clements out of jail before Esther Morris arrives from South Pass. Zeke's hoping to hear more, but you only have two or three days.'

'Puttin' on a badge wasn't part of my plans.'

The artist frowned. 'Pedlar breaks out Clements, and I think Bridgetown will be finished for decent folk.' The Englishman's mouth tightened. 'Are you just planning to ride on?'

For a few seconds Harper studied the frustration etched on the artist's face. Tom Gladwin sure had his heart in the right place, he decided. And he was a brave man. Sure, he'd volunteered to help in the arroyo. But the danger when those three no-goods were aiming to kill was over in moments. Real courage was needed to leave the comforts of the East to come out West and try to make a living with boxes of paints and stuff.

Tom Gladwin had earned the right to an answer to his question, but what the hell could he say? That he'd come to the Double M only because he'd answered a request for help from John Meeks? How could he explain that it was establishing the truth of John's death that counted above everything? Should he tell Gladwin that the problems of Bridgetown were the townsfolks', not his?

He was about to give Gladwin his answer when he saw Abby turn the corner of the barn, walking towards the big house. She was wearing a shimmering green dress and a small hat as if bound for a fancy party in town.

The late morning sun shone on her hair, contrasting with the whiteness of her long neck. The green dress was short enough for him to catch sight of her fine shoes as she stepped across the grass. Again he marvelled at the fancy clothes she wore. Then he realized these were the clothes she was wearing for the portrait Gladwin was painting.

She mounted the steps leading to the wide entrance door to the big house. Then, as he watched, she surprised him, by looking his way, and raising her hand to wave before disappearing through the doorway.

He turned away from Gladwin, and mounted his grey. 'I'm goin' into town,' he said.

Harper hitched his grey to the post in front of the Reverend Martin's clapboard which stood some fifty yards across a grassy patch from the small white-painted church. As he pushed open the low gate, the door to the house opened and the reverend stood on the step, a beaming smile on his red-cheeked face.

'You've come at exactly the right time, Mr Harper. We were just speaking of you.'

Harper shook Martin's outstretched hand. 'No harm in listenin' to what you folks gotta say,' he said.

'That's all we ask, Mr Harper.' He pointed to a low table. 'That's fine for your belt.'

Harper followed Martin into a room, surprisingly large for a parlour in a church house. Five men sat around in soft chairs. All wore city suits, the middle one who appeared to be the oldest, sported a spade-shaped black beard flecked with grey, a big gold chain gracing the blue vest beneath his black Prince Albert.

Harper took the chair offered by Martin, who then sat down on a hard-looking stool. Martin paused for a moment, and then nodded at the bearded man.

'The name's Miller, Mr Harper, and I run the bank in this town. All of us here are Bridgetown's councilmen. For this side of the bridge, that is,' he added heavily.

'Davis has gone, and he's not missed,' said the man to the banker's right. 'Forgive me, Reverend, my being in your house, but Davis was a whoremonger and I can't help wondering if he was involved with those two wretched women.'

'I'll get to it, Mr Harper,' Martin said. 'We've heard what Pedlar's planning. We desperately need a sheriff.'

'You've no other men in town?' Harper said.

'Maybe a coupla years back we could have found more than one man suitable for the job. But times have changed hereabouts. The men have settled down, brought wives from back East. They're raising children.'

The reverend sighed deeply. 'Jake Pedlar's been in Bridgetown since he was a boy. He was always ambitious. When he started his business across the bridge I confess we thought it good that he kept the miners away from decent folk. But his power has grown, Mr Harper. He seems to think he can take what he wants, and he now has gunmen to back him up. Our men can't handle that.'

'They're not lacking in courage, Mr Harper,' said the red-faced man, seated beside the reverend. 'But they need the right sort of leadership.'

Harper looked along the short line of men facing him. Their earnest, honest faces, spoke of their determination, but also of their helplessness in the face of the ruthlessness of Pedlar. Clements would be free within an hour of Pedlar's men riding across the bridge unless a real force could be put together to stop him. The rule of law in Bridgetown would be finished. Within months, maybe weeks, the town would fall apart, people would move away, and Pedlar could pick off the Double M at his leisure. Dexter would come to terms. Maybe, from what he'd seen, he already had. Abby would stand no chance.

'You're all sure the townsmen will vote me in?'

Miller gave a wry smile. 'The womenfolk, too, Mr Harper. They've had the vote hereabouts since '69.'

'You're wastin' your time if you think I can clean up the other side of the bridge,' Harper said. 'You're not gonna stop men findin' gold, an' spendin' it the way they want.'

'We know that, Mr Harper,' Miller said. 'All we ask is that this side of the bridge is kept for decent folks and we can safely go about our business. We don't imagine we can get rid of Pedlar; just keep him the other side of the bridge.' He looked around at the others. 'We can go to three hundred a month.'

There were vigorous nods of agreement from all the men around him.

Harper turned his thoughts over. Should he tell them now that he would be riding on before a month was passed? He was sure now that before long he would know the truth behind John's death, and the man responsible.

'We'll talk money later,' Harper said. 'Right now, I'll make a deal with you gentlemen,' he said. 'You'll know that Pedlar's aimin' to break out Clements. I'll wear the badge for the next few days. After Pedlar makes his move we'll talk again.'

Harper looked at the Reverend Martin, a faint smile showing on his face.

'I guess I don't have to ask if there's a Bible here for my oath,' he said.

Harper reined in, slid easily from his saddle, and hitched his grey to the post in front of the sheriff's office. He was ready now to see what he could get from Clements. He stepped up from the hardpack, his spurs sounding against the wooden boards as he went up the wide steps and pushed open the door.

The place was empty. On a desk scarred with burn

marks lay the remnants of a meal; bread, some sort of jerky, a tin cup half full of coffee. High-backed chairs faced each other across the desk. A mat, made with thin ropes lashed together, covered the space in front of the pot-bellied stove. Beyond the stove a guncase, empty of weapons, was pinned to the wall.

A door was set into the wall opposite from where Harper was standing. The door leading to the cages, he realized. He went across and pushed open the door, stepping into a narrow corridor that fronted two separate cages, one of them empty. In the other, Clements lay on the wooden cot, an arm bent over the front of his chest, his hand covering his eyes.

'You got my grub there, Wilkins?' Clements said, without moving. 'You gotta be faster next time!'

'No grub, Clements!'

Clements lifted his hand slowly from his face, shifted to swing his feet onto the floor of the cell, and looked towards Harper.

'Who the hell are you?' His eyes narrowed as he peered through the half-light. 'Goddamn! Jake's gonna kill you for puttin' me in this place, Harper! An' I ain't gonna be in here for long!'

'I hear Jake's gonna try an' break you out,' Harper said.

'An' he'll do it! The town's full of yellowbellies. Only that whore-loving bastard Davis would wear the badge. An' now he's run scared!'

'Yeah, I been thinkin' about that,' Harper said evenly. His hand dropped to rest on the butt of his Peacemaker. 'So I shoot you now, an' Jake ain't got any reason to come over here.'

Clements half rose from his cot, eyes wide open, his jaw sagging. Then he fell back, his face twisting into a sneer.

'There's only one badge in town an' that's on Wilkins.

That Bible-punching deputy ain't gonna stand by an' let you do that.'

'S'posin' the town gotta new sheriff?'

'He ain't gonna let you do that neither!'

'You wanna bet your no-good life on that?'

Harper lifted his hand from his side-arm to hold back the right side of his trail coat. The silver-coloured badge of Sheriff gleamed on the front of his woollen shirt.'

'See my problem, Clements?' Harper said evenly. 'As long as you're here alive, Jake's gonna come over the bridge an' shoot up the town. I dump your body on the bridge, an' I ain't gotta problem.'

'Fer Chris'sakes, Harper!' Clements's face worked desperately. 'We were goin' after a lousy fifty head of beeves. You gonna put me on Boot Hill for that?' His eyes flickered away from Harper. 'That high-falutin bitch from the Double M ain't gonna like that!'

'You mention Miss Forrest like that again, Clements, an' I'm gonna come in that cage and whup you.' He drew his Peacemaker, and stepped back a pace. 'I ain't puttin' you on Boot Hill for a few beeves: I'm gonna put you there for murderin' Doc Meeks.'

Clements's head jerked up.

'No, mister, no!' He shook his head vigorously. 'I swear it! I had nothin' to do with that! Doc Meeks was a good man. Fixed my arm when I got it chewed up!'

Harper felt the bile come into the back of his throat, and he swallowed quickly. Since finding the button from John's Prince Albert on Dexter's land he'd been sure that John had been murdered. But beating Clements, he suspected, would be a waste of his energies. Clements, he reckoned, hadn't enough brains to lie convincingly. But why had John been out on Dexter's land, far from any track or trail? Had Pedlar, riding to Dexter's big house, crossed John's path. But even had that happened what would cause Pedlar to kill a doctor who was well-liked on both sides of the bridge?

'You answer some of these questions, an' I'll see what I can do for you. Was it Jake? You're close to him, I hear.'

'Fer Chris'sakes, mister, don't do this!'

'Those two dead whores, Clements, they got a place in what's goin' on?'

Clements raised his head, a sudden weariness showing on his face as he looked through the bars at Harper. 'Mister, I'll tell you somethin': I ain't no longer sure what's goin' on. An' I wish I'd never been part of it.'

CHAPTER TEN

Harper looked hard at the men who stood around him in the sheriff's office. These were the men who would play the key roles in what he was planning. Money couldn't buy these men, and each had refused the deputy's bounty the council had offered. He'd be a long time forgiving himself if any of them were dead by nightfall.

Tom Gladwin looked relaxed, his Winchester held loosely down by his side. Harper wondered if the artist ever asked himself if he'd gotten more than he bargained for since he'd found himself in the cottonwoods watching Harper being beaten. Joe Jessop, thumbs tucked in his belt, his heavy Remington on his hip, leaned against the wall by the stove. An old soldier, Harper knew he could be trusted to stay calm.

Zeke's expression showed his determination to be part of what was going to happen. Harper had seen how fast he was with a gun. But how would he react if and when the shooting started? Zeke had character enough to voice his own doubts to Harper when he'd volunteered to take on Pedlar and his men. Harper had given him the words he himself had once been given.

'You'll find out if the shooting starts.'

Sam Monroe stood loose-limbed, his experience of soldiering showing in his easy manner, his long gun butt-down on the floor. Harper had been surprised when the ex-soldier had asked to join them.

'I ain't fought for what's right to stand by when somebody's tryin' to do things wrong,' he'd told Harper.

'Any you men got questions after I've said my piece, speak up,' Harper said. 'We're in this together, and I'm aimin' we come out together.'

Harper looked around at each man in turn. 'Anybody wants to walk away, nobody's gonna think any of the worse of 'em.'

He paused, giving them all a few moments to consider. Awkwardly, the men exchanged glances between them, before looking back at Harper. Again he looked at each man in turn. When nobody moved, Harper nodded.

'OK,' he said. 'I've talked already with the townsfolk. They're gonna back us. That's where Tom and Sam are gonna be the aces up our sleeve.' He looked across at both men. 'You've heard what I want. You both okay with that?'

'We're fine, Luke,' Gladwin said.

'It's my reckonin' that Pedlar and his men will check out the town first,' Harper continued. 'He tries to rush us here and townsfolk are gonna get in the way. Lotsa folks could get killed.'

'You don't think we should clear the Main Street right now?' Gladwin asked.

'It's a risk, Tom,' Harper admitted. 'But if Pedlar crosses the bridge to find the place deserted, he's gonna smell trouble.'

'Zeke's been told they're comin' over the bridge after noon,' Jessop said.

'I'm guessin', but I reckon they'll make for the saloon afore heading this way,' Harper said.

'S'posin' they do rush us here soon as they cross the bridge?' Jessop asked.

'Then we'll forget the townsmen. We can't ask men with families to fight off a siege. Sam and Tom will join us, and we'll make a stand here. We get a few of 'em afore they get any of us, and Pedlar's gonna start thinkin' maybe he ain't doin' so good.'

Again he looked around at each man. 'But I'm gonna tell you what I told the townsfolk. I'm aimin' to have Pedlar back across that bridge without a shot bein' fired. The townsfolk here ain't gonna take heart from havin' a gun battle on Main Street.'

As he finished speaking, the door opened and Wilkins, the elderly deputy who'd run errands for Davis stepped in. A small man with a prominent chin above a stiff white collar, he'd only agreed to keep watch when Harper threatened to take away his badge and the money that went with it. On Harper's orders, he'd been keeping watch since daybreak in case Pedlar came over the bridge earlier than expected.

'Mr Harper, reckon I should tell you,' Wilkins said, in a voice which quavered slightly, 'coupla tough-lookin' strangers just rode into town. One of 'em's a tall mean-lookin' feller, with big moustaches and a cannon like yourn on his hip.' Wilkins took off his hat and scratched his head. 'Mighty strange, though. Other feller's gotta little gel on a pony ridin' with him.'

'Mr Wilkins,' Harper said, 'we had more time, I'd buy you a bottle!'

He strode to the door and flung it open as William Bolden reached the hitching post outside the office. Bolden looked across at Harper, his eyes lingering on the badge pinned to Harper's vest.

'I knew you was gonna be trouble, Mr Harper, first time I set eyes on you.' He turned to Frank Jackson who was leading his daughter Lucy's pony to the hitching post.

'Seems we ridden all this way, Frank, to find Mr Harper already got what we came for.'

Harper grinned. 'Good to see you, Mr Bolden. You sure picked the right time.'

Bolden shifted in his saddle. 'Knowin' you Mr Harper, that means me and Frank are maybe gonna get shot at.'

Harper's grin broadened. 'Goes with the star, Mr Bolden. An' by tomorrow the badge'll be yourn, anyways.'

'You sayin' that, I guess we'll stay 'round,' Bolden said. He swung down from his horse. 'We gotta place for Lucy?'

'Widow Henry's place,' said Jessop, who'd come to stand by Harper. 'First right after the dry goods.'

'Get Lucy settled, Frank,' Bolden said. 'I'll find out what we got ourselves into.'

Five minutes later, having taken a look at Clements who raised himself briefly from the wooden cot to peer at his visitors, Bolden was sipping coffee, poured from the black-ened pot which sat atop the stove. He listened intently while Harper explained the situation.

'Pedlar's takin' helluva gamble,' Bolden said, putting down the tin mug on Harper's desk. 'Folks down in Cheyenne get to hear of this, they ain't gonna take kindly tryin' to break a man outa jail.'

'There's somethin' goin' on in this town I still ain't gotta handle on,' Harper admitted. 'I reckoned at first that Clements was too dumb to hide anything. But now I'm beginning to wonder. Maybe Pedlar's worried he'll talk.'

'OK. How many men you reckon Pedlar will bring.'

'Twelve, maybe fourteen.'

'An' reckonin' he'll go in the saloon first, how many you got goin' in with you?'

'Two, Joe Jessop and Zeke here.'

Bolden leaned back in his chair, and blew air threw pursed lips.

'You crazy sonovabitch,' he said.

The door opened, and Frank Jackson stepped in.

'Lucy's OK,' he said, looking around at the grimfaced men. 'What we gotta do?'

'We gotta say our prayers, Frank,' Bolden said. 'That's what we gotta do.'

Harper looked up at the clock pinned to the whitewashed wall above his chair. Ten after noon.

'You think he ain't comin'?' Zeke asked, his voice hoarse.

'He'll come,' said Harper, and turned to see Wilkins step through the doorway.

'Pedlar an' his men just gone into the Paradise,' Wilkins said, his voice shaky.

'How many?'

'Dozen maybe.'

'OK, Wilkins. No need for you to hang on 'round here.'

Harper waited until Wilkins had closed the door, the sound of his footsteps retreating along the boardwalk, before he turned to the group of men, all standing now.

'Tom, Sam, over to the livery,' Harper said. 'Don't forget the bandannas.'

'Sure thing, Sheriff,' said Monroe.

Both men went through the door into the corridor which led past the cages to the rear of the building. Harper turned to Jackson.

'Frank, you're gonna stay here with the scattergun. Anybody from Pedlar makes it to either door you know what to do. We'll shout loud and clear if it's one of us comin' in. You comfortable with that?'

Jackson nodded and held up his weapon, a double-

barrelled hammer shotgun with the butt cut down to the
pistol grip, its barrel only a foot long.

'But remember, we're aimin' to keep it peaceful,'
Harper said, turning to the others. 'Nobody draws a
sidearm when we go in. I ain't riskin' a bloodbath.'

'S'posin' one of them does go for his gun?' Jessop
asked.

'That's why we got Zeke with us. Me an' Mr Bolden
draw our Peacemakers, an' Pedlar's gonna reckon he's in
a war, an' start shootin'.' Harper paused, thinking his plan
through. 'Time we get into the saloon, I guess they'll be
feelin' easy, maybe reckonin' bustin' out Clements is
gonna be easy pickin's.'

He breathed in deeply. 'We're gonna stop 'em,' he said.

On the hardpack of Main Street, Harper turned his head
to glance at the group of men standing near the corner of
the livery. Satisfied, he looked up to the doorway of the
Paradise, sucking oxygen into his lungs.

'Here we go,' he said.

He went up the steps and through the doorway of the
saloon. Bolden, now wearing a badge like the rest, was
close behind, Joe Jessop and Zeke bringing up the rear.
The midday sun threw light over their shoulders, illumi-
nating the interior of the saloon around the bar. Once
inside, the four men fanned out, making a line to face the
bar. Harper stood maybe a couple of paces in front of the
others.

A dozen men had their backs to him, their voices loud,
hoarse laughter sounding around the saloon. A stranger
walking into the bar might have thought it was better to
take a drink elsewhere. Beyond them, an anxious Shorty
moved to and fro, a whiskey bottle in his hand, filling
glasses. In the centre of the line, Pedlar stood straight,

boots gleaming, the silver on his spurs sparkling in the sun's rays.

'Finish your drink, Pedlar. Then take your men back across the bridge,' Harper said loudly.

There was a sudden silence. Slowly, heads turned, and twelve pairs of eyes came to rest on Harper. There was a muttered oath, and one of the men at the bar reached for his sidearm. His hand froze on the butt as Zeke's Navy Colt, held at arm's length, aimed directly for his heart.

Pedlar, who had turned fully around to face Harper, leaned his back against the bar. The corners of his mouth lifted in a grim smile.

'Goddammit, Harper, you sure are a passel of trouble to me. Shoulda killed you that first day. You must be the hardest dollar I ever earned.'

'No shootin', Pedlar. We'll settle our differences elsewhere. Just you and me. Nobody goes for his gun, and Zeke'll put away his iron.'

He paused until he was sure nobody in front of him was about to make a move. Iron slid against leather as Zeke reholstered his Colt.

The two lines of men faced each other. Nobody moved, nobody said anything. If he made a wrong move now, Harper thought, this is going to finish in the men alongside him getting killed. But he knew the time was right to make his play. Both Tom Gladwin and Sam Monroe would be in position by now.

'I'm gonna say it again, Pedlar. Finish your drink an' get back across the bridge.'

The smile disappeared from Pedlar's face, the angular face tautening with rage. 'You reckon on givin' me orders, Harper?' Pedlar shouted. 'You think that tin star is gonna stop me from buryin' you?'

Pedlar's stare shifted from Harper to Bolden. 'You're a

stranger here, mister. Don't get tangled up in somethin' that ain't your business.'

'I'm makin' it my business,' Bolden said.

'You gotta big mouth, stranger.'

If Pedlar thought he could push Bolden into making a wrong move he was mistaken. Bolden merely showed his large teeth in a wolfish smile.

Pedlar looked left and right at the men alongside him, then back to Harper. 'I got a dozen men here. A man gets hisself killed, an' his money goes in the pot. You got an old man, a kid who thinks he's fast, an' a stranger. You wanna figure the odds?'

'I've already figured 'em,' Harper said evenly. 'You wanna take a look out front?'

Pedlar frowned, obviously puzzled by Harper's remarks. He pushed himself off the bar to walk to the window overlooking Main Street. Harper stepped forward to halt alongside him.

'Sonovabitch!' Pedlar swore aloud.

On the hardpack of Main Street, beyond the dozen horses lined up at the rail, a wagon had been turned on its side. The heavy boarding provided protection for ten men. Each man had a long gun at his shoulder, five men aiming at the door of the saloon, five aiming at the saloon's window. Each man's face was covered from nose to chin in a bandanna, giving them the threatening appearance of masked attackers.

Pedlar swung on his heel. 'Kansas! Check the back.'

A man broke from the line, went around the back of the bar, shoving Shorty out of the way to throw open the door to the back of the saloon. He slammed it shut immediately.

'Fer Chris'sakes, Jake! There's raiders out there! They got a wagon—'

'Shut your goddamned mouth!' Jake yelled, frustration boiling over in his voice.

He stamped his way across the sawdust-covered floor to the bar, and downed his whiskey in one gulp. Then he swung around on Harper.

'You're gonna die real slow, Harper. An' I'm gonna do it myself!'

Harper felt his muscles twitch with anticipation. 'It's your call, Pedlar!'

He could see on Pedlar's face the struggle that was going on in the man's mind. Sure, he could risk a gunfight in the saloon. But with twenty armed men at the front and back of the saloon his chances of survival were small.

Pedlar jerked his head at his men. 'We're gonna go back!'

'Not so fast, Pedlar!' Harper rapped out. 'Your men go one at a time. You go last when I tell you. Any of your men draws his sidearm this side of the bridge and I'll shoot you down.'

When he registered the look that came into Pedlar's eyes, he thought he'd overplayed his hand. For an instant his hand went to the butt of his Peacemaker, aware that Bolden had made the same move.

Hatred gleamed in Pedlar's eyes but his hands stayed by his sides.

'Fletcher, you first!' Pedlar ordered.

'I ain't likin' this, boss!'

'Shut your mouth an' do as you're goddamned told!'

As the man named Fletcher reluctantly began to move across the saloon, Joe Jessop stepped quickly to the doorway.

'They're comin' out!' He called to Tom Gladwin, hidden behind his bandanna. 'Hold your fire!'

Harper didn't move, his hand resting lightly on the butt

of his sidearm as each of Pedlar's men filed out of the saloon and mounted his horse. He gave each man a few minutes to ride towards the bridge before ordering the next to follow.

Finally, Pedlar was the only one left. Harper followed him from the saloon and stood on the boardwalk outside his office while Pedlar mounted his big roan.

Pedlar glared at Harper, hatred in his eyes. 'I ain't the only one after your hide, Harper. But I'm gonna be the first to nail it!'

With a hard pull at his horse's head, and a cruel jab of his spurs, Pedlar urged his mount forward in the direction of the bridge.

For a few seconds Harper stood still, his hand resting easily on the butt of his Peacemaker, watching Pedlar's mount stirring up the dust of Main Street. His mind turned over that final snarled threat. Just what the hell did Pedlar mean by that?

CHAPTER ELEVEN

'I reckon I might well give up this painting game, and become a gunfighter,' said Tom Gladwin loudly, his voice blurred with the half-a-dozen whiskies he'd drunk in the past hour.

There was a roar of laughter around the table from the band of men who had forced Pedlar to ride back into his own territory over the bridge.

'Here's to Tom Gladwin, the fastest draw in the West!' Harper said, raising his glass. 'With a paintbrush,' he added.

Again there were shouts of laughter, the tension of the standoff seeping away as the bottles, bought by the townsmen who had crowded into the saloon to express their thanks, were steadily emptied.

Shorty, who'd been happy to act as table servant for an hour or more, moved around the table, refilling glasses. William Bolden held up his hand in a gesture of refusal.

'No more whiskey for me, Shorty. Me and Frank here, we got work to do.'

Harper, too, got to his feet. He unpinned the star from his vest. 'I'm obliged to you, Mr Bolden. You've heard what the councilmen said; the reverend's waiting to swear you in.'

Bolden took the star. 'Reckon you an' me ain't seen the

last of trouble for a while,' he said. His grin was broad beneath his moustaches. 'This sure beats collecting taxes in Plainville!'

'Me an' Sam'll check the long guns over at the jail-house,' Harper said. 'Sam can bring you the keys.'

Joe Jessop looked at Zeke and Tom Gladwin, both of whom were lolling back in their chairs, clutching their glasses, amiable smiles wreathing their faces.

'We'll ride back to the Double M. I'll keep an eye on these two sportin' gentlemen!'

'Good thinkin', Joe,' Harper said. 'Could be the hard-est work you've done today!' He looked around at the barkeeper. 'Thanks, Shorty. Let's go, Sam.'

Harper led the way out of the saloon, both men acknowledging the shouts of congratulations from the other side of Main Street. A young woman carrying a basket covered with a cloth smiled up at Harper from beneath her bonnet.

'This will be a good town to live in again, Mr Harper,' she said.

Harper smiled, and touched a finger to his hat. He hoped the young woman was right. Pedlar was probably planning his next move even as she'd spoken. Bolden had a point. It wasn't over yet.

He and Monroe went up to the boardwalk and entered the sheriff's office. Harper took a key from his vest pocket and unlocked the guncase, newly stocked with weapons. Together, both men inspected the long guns, unloading each one, and setting aside those which would need clean-ing.

Wordlessly they worked alongside each other for maybe half an hour. Then, busy with a rag soaked in oil, Monroe looked up at Harper who was counting ammunition.

'Makes me think of the days in the 54th,' he said.

Harper looked up quickly, his mind switching from his examination of the barrel of a .44 Winchester.

'You say the 54th, Sam?'

'Sho' did. Spent a lot of the War with Colonel Shaw. God rest his soul.'

'You remember the surgeon?'

'Doc Meeks?' Monroe chuckled. 'Gave the Colonel a helluva time! Used to ride with us up to the line.' Monroe paused, his face suddenly serious. 'Mighty useful tho', a man got a Johnny Reb slug.'

His smile returned. 'Yo' sayin Doc Meeks 'round these parts?'

Harper shook his head. 'He was. He died a few weeks back.'

'Now that's a real shame.' Monroe closed his eyes for a moment. 'The Lord rest his soul.' He blew out air through ballooned cheeks. 'Ain't that the way of the world? A fine man like Doc Meeks cashes in his chips, an' that scallywag Cap'n Elliott walks 'round bolder'n brass.'

Harper put down the Winchester on the desk. 'I ain't followin' you, Sam. You sayin' an officer once in the 54th is here in Bridgetown?'

Monroe nodded. 'Sho' is, Mr Harper. Saw him with my own eyes.' He wrinkled his nose at what he seemed to consider a lack of justice in the world. 'A man like that should hide his face from decent folks.'

Harper leaned across and took the long gun Monroe was working on.

'Sam, put down that cleanin' stuff you got there. Tell me about this Elliott.'

Monroe glanced up at the daub and wattle covering the timbers of the roof above him, marshalling his thoughts.

'Middle o' '63, I reckon. We was well to the north of Charleston, mebbe a day or two's march to the harbour.

Nobody could work it out how she did it, but this sassy gal found out where her man was, an' caught up with us when we stopped outside the town. Got into his tent, an' all, some of the men saw her, an' all hell broke out. Her man got taken away for a lashing, an' she got took off to Cap'n Elliott.' He screwed his eyes shut for a moment. When he opened them he looked away from Harper and out through the window overlooking Main Street.

'Truth of the matter is, Mr Harper, I gotta admit it. I was the sergeant who took her to Cap'n Elliott. If I hadn't they'd have taken my stripes and given me a lashin'.'

He paused, his face showing the memory of what happened still haunted him. 'She was a stupid black gel, but she shoulda got better.'

'What happened, Sam?'

'We found her body on the road next day when we was leavin'.'

'An' you think this Captain Elliott knew somethin'?'

'I cain't say fer sure, Mr Harper. Coupla days later we was at Battery Wagner an' I'd other things on my mind. Anyways, Cap'n Elliott was officers' business. All I do know is a coupla weeks later the new colonel kicked him outa the 54th. An' folks did tell that he was drummed outa the army.'

'An' you've seen Elliott in Bridgetown. When was that?'

Monroe frowned. 'First day I got here, I reckon. Saw him comin' outa the dry goods store, makin' for the bridge.'

'What did this Elliott look like?'

Monroe shrugged. 'Ordinary sorta feller, I guess. Tall, trail clothes, nothin' special.'

Harper put his hand beneath his trail shirt and took a handful of coins from the pouch he carried. 'Sam, nobody saw your face today. I want you to go across the bridge.

Find where this Elliott's livin', an' come see me back at the Double M. You willin' to do that?'

'Sho', Mr Harper.' He glanced at the coins in Harper's outstretched hand. 'But I ain't needin' all that!'

Harper closed Monroe's fist over the money. 'Take it. You need more, I'll give you more. You find Elliott, Sam, an' if what I'm thinkin' is right, we're gonna know everythin' that's been goin' on 'round here.'

'Come on through, Mr Harper,' Dr Scott said. 'The townsfolk are in your debt after today.'

'I was gonna ride to the Double M,' Harper explained. 'Shorty said you wanted to see me.'

'I certainly did, Mr Harper.' Scott waved to the chair opposite the desk.

A smile lit up his face, wrinkling the lines of tiredness at the corner of his eyes. 'I've good news for Miss Abigail. I think Dan Roper is going to be fine. His wound is healing again.' He hesitated. 'Although I'm not sure if it's my doctoring or Roper's good luck.'

'I'll tell Miss Abby when I get back. This is the good news she's been waiting for.' Harper picked up his hat from the floor beside his chair and stood up.

Scott clapped a hand to his head. 'Oh my goodness! My mind is in a whirl, Mr Harper! That's what I had to tell you! Roper is desperate to speak with you.'

Harper frowned. 'He doesn't even know me.'

'He knows of you, Mr Harper. And he says he saw something you'll want to know about.'

'Then you'd better take me to him, Doc.'

Scott jumped up from his seat. 'He's through the back. I have a couple of rooms when I need to keep someone.'

Harper followed the doctor through a short corridor and into a room set up for the care of the sick. On a long narrow table were cloths and instruments. A large china pot stood at the end. Two buckets, each covered with a thick cloth, stood by a wall. On a small table against a side wall, a sheaf of paper, and a pen were readily available, Harper assumed, for Scott to take notes on his patients' conditions.

As the two men entered a young woman stood up from the chair in the corner of the room. She wore a long white apron over her blue cotton dress, and her hair was tied up in a cloth.

'Take a break, Mary,' Scott said. 'I'll be here for a little while.'

The two men waited until she'd left before they approached the bed at the far end of the room where Roper was propped up against thick pillows. A rough grey blanket, over sheets, covered the bed as far as his stomach. Above the edge of the sheet, bandages were wrapped around his chest, a thick pad showing its shape on the right-hand side of Roper's chest.

'Dan?' Scott said softly. 'Mr Harper's here.'

Roper, a fair-haired man in his mid-twenties opened his eyes, his mouth curving in a brief smile. With obvious effort, he moved himself on the thick pillows supporting his back.

'Take it easy now, Dan,' Scott said.

'That's okay, Doc. I gotta talk with Mr Harper.' He looked up. 'You are Mr Harper, ain't you?'

Harper could just hear him without bending towards the bed. 'Doc Scott tells me you're a lucky man. You're gonna be fine.'

Roper nodded, the faint smile reappearing. 'The Ropers are tough,' he said. 'But I gotta tell you, Mr Harper, 'bout the day I got shot.'

'Go ahead, Dan, take your time.'

'The day I got shot I saw Doc Meeks out at the Dexter spread.'

'Are you sure, Dan?' Scott said. 'We used to go out there regularly,' he added, addressing Harper. 'One of the house servants has a boy with consumption and John wanted me familiar with the condition.' He pursed up his mouth. 'But it was unusual for John to visit alone.'

Roper shook his head vigorously. 'No, Doc! I guess I ain't tellin' this right.'

Scott put a hand on Roper's shoulder. 'Take it easy, Dan.'

'Just tell us how it was,' Harper said. 'Take your time.'

'I'd been chasin' strays. We got some fifty head of beeves on the other side of the river,' Roper said. 'They're young an' some of 'em stray. I was up on the Dexter spread, when I saw this feller standin' by his horse. Them Dexter fellers can be a mite unfriendly, so I took shelter in a stand of trees.'

Roper paused, as if summoning up more strength. 'I was curious so I took out my old spyglass to get a good look at what this feller was doin'.'

Roper leaned forward an inch from the pillow. 'Mr Harper, it was Doc Meeks, an' he was diggin' with a spade. Right out there in the middle of nowhere!'

'He must have found a special plant or flower,' said Scott.

'What happened next?' Harper asked.

'Three riders appeared, an' the doc' went with 'em.'

'Dexter's men?'

'His or that Jake Pedlar's. I didn't know any of 'em.' Roper said. 'I was watchin' 'em ride away when I got shot. The critter musta sneaked up on me.'

Harper thought for a moment. 'You got shot the same day as Doc Meeks was found dead?'

'That's right, Mr Harper.' Roper, agitated now, tried to

push himself further off the pillow. 'An' that ain't all. I knowed I got shot on the Dexter spread, but Mr Jessop said they found me by the river on the Double M side!'

'Take it easy, Dan,' Scott said again. He glanced at Harper and shook his head slightly.

'I'm obliged to you, Dan,' Harper said. 'I'll tell Miss Abby you're gonna be fine. Now you get some sleep.'

Back in Scott's study, the doctor looked hard at Harper.

'You don't think John was digging for a plant?'

Harper shook his head. 'No, Doc. I'm thinkin' he was diggin' for that girl Janey.'

Harper held his grey to a steady lope heading for the Double M. The wind stirred the animal's mane, and Harper pulled down more firmly on his hat. The sun dropping in the sky to the west cast long shadows across the bunch and buffalo grass either side of the beaten-down ground of the track.

What a hell of a day it had been. His lips pulled back from his teeth in a wry smile. His life hadn't been this crazy since those days down on the Mexican border. Maybe he was beginning to take too many risks. Was he going to end up like so many of the men he had known, face down in the dirt, past the time when they might have put away their gun?

Maybe he should have stayed in Boston, worn a city suit, attended church on Sunday, gone to college and studied law or something, led the life his stepfather had once hoped for him, instead of hightailing it out West.

What were those last words he'd said to Harper when he'd left for the railroad? 'You're chasing shadows, son.' When he thought back over the years he supposed he had found a shadow. But maybe his kinfolk would say it was the shadow of the gun.

Maybe it really was the time to go back to his roots, and drop the frontier way of speech he'd adopted like so many other Easterners who had made the journey westwards. He could take off his trail clothes for the last time, buy city suits, read a proper newspaper, spend time looking at the pictures Tom Gladwin was always talking about. The notion was worth thinking more about. The problem with that notion was that he couldn't see any place for Abby.

The blood gushed from the grey's neck six inches from Harper's leg. The crack of the shot reached him an instant later. He threw himself forward, kicking his heels from his stirrups, rolling from the saddle as his mount collapsed beneath him. His hat went flying into the dust as the momentum of his roll sent him crashing into the dust, turning him over and over down the slope of the ground that fell away from the track.

He dug a boot heel into the ground to stop his slide, his Peacemaker already out, firing in three directions as he swung the sidearm to and fro, not expecting to hit anyone, for he knew the shot that had hit his grey came from a rifle, but to deter anyone from closing in.

He lay there, his eyes scanning the slight inclines of the land, and the small stand of trees from where, he guessed, the shooter had fired. He held his breath and strained to hear any movement above the gentle whisper of the wind. There! From beyond the trees came the fading sound of a single horse's hoofs at the gallop.

Harper scrabbled across the ground towards his grey. Blood was pouring from the animal, its eyes rolling, its forelegs kicking feebly against the dirt of the track. Avoiding the animal's hoofs, Harper dug into his saddle-bag.

Satisfied that he had spare ammunition, he turned his Peacemaker to aim at the animal's head. He'd ridden too many different horses in the last years to be sentimental, but in the short time since he'd bought the animal down in Cheyenne he'd come to depend on the grey.

'You sonovabitch, Pedlar!' Harper said softly. And pulled the trigger.

CHAPTER TWELVE

Three days had passed since Harper, carrying his saddle and his Winchester, had limped around the barn of the Double M, past the corral under the gaze of Joe Jessop, and entered the cabin to be greeted by an astonished Tom Gladwin.

Ten minutes later, a concerned Abigail Forrest had sent her girl to discover what was going on, and then, having learned of the attempt on Harper's life, had come across to the cabin herself to insist that both men join her for supper. That evening, as Harper and Gladwin had sat with Abby around the large mahogany table, Harper had almost persuaded himself that it had been worth getting shot at.

Now Harper was in the big house once more, again with Abby and Tom Gladwin. He and Abby were sitting at one end of the largest room in the house waiting for Gladwin to unveil the portrait of Abby he'd been working on. Neither Abby nor Harper had so far been allowed to see the results of Gladwin's work.

Abby's cheeks were pink with anticipation, and Harper was surprised to detect in her brown eyes the signs of nervousness. Maybe his eyes showed the same. Walking into that saloon to face Pedlar, he reckoned, was a damned sight easier than waiting for Tom to pull aside the cloth

120

covering the painting. For Abby's sake more than for the artist's, he was wishing fervently that the portrait would be a success.

'Seems we're over the worst,' he said, intent on having her think of something else while Gladwin fiddled around with a cloth. Was Tom going to take for ever?

'Roper is on the mend; Bolden's got his side of the bridge under control; an' we've seen nothin' of Pedlar's men on the Double M.'

'And that's because of you,' she said, her eyes shining with pleasure.

Harper shook his head. 'Tom, Joe Jessop, young Zeke, Sam, William Bolden, they were all there when it counted. An' let's not forget the townsmen.'

'But you made it happen, Luke,' she said.

It was the first time she'd used his forename, and he might have said something foolish if right at that moment Gladwin hadn't turned their way.

'A portrait by Mr Thomas Gladwin, of London, England!' Gladwin announced, standing stiffly alongside the hidden painting, propped on its makeshift easel.

'I present Miss Abigail Forrest,' he said with a flourish, and pulled off the cloth to disclose the portrait.

For almost thirty seconds there was absolute silence in the room. Then Abby clapped her hands together.

'Oh! Tom! I think it's wonderful,' she said, emotion suddenly catching at her throat.

'Abby's right, Tom,' Harper said. 'You've done fine work.'

You've painted her as beautiful as she is in life, he added mentally, and if sometime in the future he was ever bold enough to say that aloud to her, he had to choose a better time than this.

Gladwin bowed low in their direction, a broad smile

stretching across his face as he straightened. 'Thank you, Miss Abby. I'm pleased with the work, too. Now where shall we hang it?'

Abby pointed to a space on the wall where cords hung down awaiting the portrait. The Englishman picked up the painting and stepped across to the wall.

'Excellent!' Gladwin said. He reached up and carefully attached the cords. 'The painting will need framing, of course. But it'll be safe here.'

He stood back, appraising it with a critical eye, his fmgers tugging at his lower lip. Then he nodded, obviously pleased. 'Better, I think, than the work I did for Clay Dexter.'

Gladwin turned around to look at Harper, his expression showing that he'd suddenly recalled something he wished to say.

'By the way, Luke, you were asking about Thomas Durant.'

'The name Luke mentioned that startled Clay Dexter?' Abby said.

Gladwin nodded. 'I only remembered yesterday. Durant is in the railroad business. He's an important man in Union Pacific.'

Harper, who until that moment had been paying more attention to the portrait than to Gladwin, was suddenly still.

'Maybe that's the answer!' Harper said, his voice almost raised to a shout. 'The railroad!'

Harper saw Gladwin and Abby exchange puzzled glances.

'Listen! UP are plannin' spurs all over the country! They were raisin' money for 'em when I was back East. Just supposin' they're plannin' one 'round here. One that crosses the Double M. The land would be worth a fortune!'

'There's an awful lot of supposing there, Luke,' Gladwin said.

Harper turned on his heel to pace across the room, the portrait forgotten.

'Why would Jake Pedlar keep on threatenin' the Double M, rustlin', shooting at the hands?'

'Hoping that Miss Abby, a woman alone, would give up and he'd get land and cattle at a knockdown price?' Gladwin said.

Harper shook his head, remembering Ruby Moreton's words about paying off Pedlar.

'Pedlar's no rancher. He uses his gunnies to take money from where he can. Anyone gets in his way, he kills. Remember what he said the other day? About me bein' a hard dollar for him to earn, and somebody else bein' after my hide?'

'Pedlar could still be after the Double M,' Abby said, 'If you were right about the UP spur, he'd make money from the railroad.'

Harper smacked his clenched fist into the palm of his other hand.

'But s'posin' he doesn't know 'bout the spur?' Harper looked hard at the other two. 'Sure, he's bein' paid to cause trouble, but maybe he only knows half of what's goin' on!'

'So who's he working for?' Gladwin asked. 'Somebody back East?'

Harper shook his head. 'He's workin' for Clay Dexter.'

'That's nonsense, Luke,' she said sharply. 'Clay Dexter saved us from Pedlar and his men out at Pioneers' Camp.'

'I been thinkin' about that. What happens to the Double M if you die?'

'The lawyers take over. They hold the land until Charlie reaches manhood.'

'Dexter wasn't saving us,' Harper said. 'Pedlar went crazy out there. Dexter had to step in to save you!' Harper looked into her eyes. 'You'd have died that day, fightin' to the end. I know it. And so did Dexter.'

Silk rustled as Abigail Forrest slowly sank into the cushioned chair, her face drained of colour. Harper could see that she'd been shaken by the notion that her neighbour, always courteous, apparently honest, was aiming to drive her from a ranch which had been in her family for so many years.

'Luke, there's something wrong,' Gladwin said. 'A lot of what you say rests on Clay Dexter learning about the spur from Thomas Durant.'

'Go on, Tom,' Harper said.

'I agree that someone else is trying to kill you. After the business in the saloon Pedlar will not be satisfied with a rifle shot from a distance.'

'I'm listenin', Tom,' Harper said.

'But everything you've said about Clay Dexter could apply to this Captain Elliott, seen by Sam. I think you must be right that one man is behind all the trouble, and we've agreed it's not Pedlar. He could be working for Elliott not Clay Dexter.'

'The two murdered girls,' said Abigail softly. 'And the Charleston girl Sam talked about.'

'And Elliott served with Dr Meeks whom you think was murdered,' Gladwin added.

For a few seconds Harper was silent, his thoughts churning. He was about to answer when there came a knock at the door. It opened to show an anxious-looking Joe Jessop standing by Abby's girl.

'Miss Abby! We can't find Charlie!'

Abigail Forrest stood up abruptly. 'Has he not returned from the schoolroom?'

'Zeke went lookin'. Charlie ain't been to school, so the schoolmarm says.'

'But didn't Zeke ride in with him this morning?'

'Yes, ma'am. Left him on the edge of town as usual.'

Abby clutched at Harper's arm. Her knuckles were white.

'You don't think. . . ?' Her voice trailed away.

'Take it easy, Abby,' Harper said, reassuringly. 'He wouldn't be the first youngster to duck outa school. I reckon I can find him. Tom'll talk to you about the picture until I get back.'

Five minutes later he was astride the horse he'd bought from Jessop and was heading for the meadow Zeke had pointed out to him on his first arrival at the Double M. Young Charlie needed his britches whipping, he decided. And once Charlie was safe at home he reckoned Abby was more than likely to administer the punishment herself.

The sounds of hoofs made him look up sharply. Who the hell was that coming towards him at a gallop? He slowed his mount from a lope to a gentle trot as the rider, head down, raced towards him. The rider must have seen Harper at about the same time, for he held up his hand in a gesture of recognition.

William Bolden. What was he getting all fired up about? Surely Pedlar hadn't made another move over the bridge? Harper reined in as Bolden halted his mount beside him.

'Fire ragin' in Bridgetown, Mr Bolden?'

The grim expression on Bolden's face didn't alter. 'Miss Abby up at the Double M? I gotta get some advice on the law.'

'What the hell's wrong?'

'That no-good Clement strung hisself up in his cell. Used his damned belt. Here!' Bolden thrust a dirty scrap of paper into Harper's hand.

The misspelled words, the letters heavily pressed onto the paper, appeared to have been written with the damp stub-end of a pencil, but their meaning was clear.

'Sory I kilt doc meeks'

Harper felt his face grow cold. The green plant stain, the whore's brooch, Roper's account of what he'd seen, now this scrap of paper. His stomach knotted at the thought that John's murderer had been in front of his Peacemaker. An hour ago he thought he'd worked out what was going on. Now, it seemed, he had to face the hard truth. All his thinking had been wrong.

He handed the scrap of paper back to Bolden. 'Miss Abby's there with Tom Gladwin,' he said.

'You comin' back?'

Harper shook his head. 'Later. Miss Abby's worried about Charlie. He's out fishin', I reckon.'

Bolden nodded, turned his mount's head, and kicked the animal forward, heading for the Double M big house at speed.

Twenty minutes later, Harper crested a ridge and walked his horse through the rich grass of the meadow. Ahead of him, the lake sparkled in the midday sun like stars in a blue velvet sky. He could hear mallards among the rushes at the lakeside. At first, a fold of ground over to the right obscured his vision, but when he was halfway down to the water he saw a solitary figure sitting on a large stone a few feet from the water's edge. A long fishpole stretched out across the water.

'Howdy, pardner,' Harper said, as he slid from the saddle to sit on the grass.

Charlie looked up, and then away from Harper.

'Howdy, Mr Harper.'

'Your marmee was worried.'

'I'm OK,' Charlie said defiantly.

'Sure you are. Only your Marmee didn't know that.' Harper broke off a stem of grass and put it in his mouth. 'Sure is a great day for fishin'.' He leaned back on his elbows. 'You given up on school?'

'Just given up on a friend,' the boy said mournfully.

Harper gave a low whistle. 'That's tough, Charlie. A man should have lotsa friends. Wanna tell me what happened?'

The boy shrugged. 'We were going to ride back from school together.'

'An' he changed his mind?'

'Not a he, Mr Harper. She's really nice, but she didn't even come to school. Her pa said she was sick but I didn't believe him.'

'Ladies change their minds, Charlie. You'll learn that.'

Charlie shook his head vigorously. 'Lucy gave me her word she'd ride with me.'

'Like I said, Charlie, ladies—' Harper broke off, snatching the grass from his mouth, and sitting up.

'Lucy who, Charlie?'

'Lucy Jackson. Her papa's the new deputy.'

With a sudden thrust of his legs, Harper uncoiled and stood, looking down at the boy.

'Charlie, I want you to ride back now to your marmee and Mr Gladwin. Tell them I'm gonna be some time. You got that?'

Charlie scrunched up his nose. 'You mean right now? I'm sure to catch more fish.'

'I mean right now, Charlie.'

The boy made a mouth but nodded, and swung his fish-pole away from the water. 'I'm on my way, Mr Harper.'

*

127

Harper stepped down from his horse as two men in dark city clothes with sombre faces beneath billycock hats came out of the sheriff's office. Undertakers, Harper guessed. He hitched his mount to the rail and went up to the office.

Frank Jackson was sitting behind the desk, looking down at a sheet of paper. His face was strained, and he was fiddling with the pen from the inkwell near his elbow. He looked up as Harper closed the door behind him.

'Howdy, Frank,' Harper said, taking the chair by the desk.

'Mr Harper,' Frank said, his voice low.

'Sheriff told me about Clements.'

'A bad business, Mr Harper,' Frank said his voice still low. 'Kinda takes it away from what we did the other day.'

'That it does, Frank.' Harper said. 'How's Lucy?'

Harper watched impassively as Frank's face lost more colour, the deputy's mouth opening and closing wordlessly.

'She's fine,' he said finally.

'You sure about that?'

'I'm sure.' Frank stared defiantly across the desk at Harper. 'She's at Widow Henry's, right now. Go see, you don't believe me.'

Harper nodded, fishing beneath his shirt to take out a small muslin bag of Bull Durham. He fished out a couple of papers, and started a couple of cigarettes, aware that the deputy was staring fixedly at his every move.

When both were finished, he handed one across to the deputy, and set fire to both with a match taken from his vest pocket. Still Harper said nothing as smoke drifted above the heads of the two men.

'When did they bring her back, Frank?' Harper said finally.

The deputy opened his mouth then shut it like a trap,

his head bowing until his chin almost touched his shirt.

'Fer Chris'sakes,' he said finally. 'I been with Mr Bolden for seven years, now I'm in this barrel o' tar.'

'Tell me what happened, Frank.'

'Two men an' a woman. They told me I'd never see Lucy alive agin.' His head came up but he looked away from Harper. 'I gave 'em the key to Clements's cell, an' took a walk. That was last night. Lucy was left at the widder's place this mornin'.'

'Were they Pedlar's men or Clay Dexter's?'

Frank looked up at Harper, surprised. 'Pedlar's men, I guess.' His eyes shifted to the paper on the desk before him.

'I was tryin' to get it on paper for Mr Bolden. I ain't sure I can tell it to his face.'

Harper leaned across the desk and picked up the paper, crumpling it into a ball. 'Lucy's worth ten of Clements,' he said. 'They had you 'cross a barrel, an' plenty of folks woulda done the same.'

'But I gotta be honest with Mr Bolden!'

'Sure you gotta be straight, but maybe later when times are easy 'round here.' Harper stood up from his chair. 'Makes sense for me to ask Pedlar some questions.' His hand dropped to the butt of his sidearm. 'Pedlar wants another chance to kill me. I'm gonna give him one!'

CHAPTER THIRTEEN

Wolf River Jack, the livery man on Pedlar's side of the bridge, fathered by a Scottish trapper and brought into this world by a Shoshone woman, both long since dead, had lit a couple of lamps and was rubbing the sleep out of his eyes when he felt the barrel of a gun pressing hard against the back of his neck. He stood very still, the tin cup slipping from his fingers, splattering coffee onto the straw-covered floor, and over the muddy toes of his black boots.

'There ain't a dollar in the whole place, mister, whoever you are,' he wheezed. 'An' I ain't carried a gun since the War.' His Adam's apple bobbed as he swallowed hard. 'An' no knives neither, save what I need for the hosses.'

'Don't turn 'round, old man,' Harper said.

'Don't get riled, mister. I ain't movin'.'

'Who you expectin' this time of day?' Harper said, lowering his Peacemaker and easing it back into its holster.

'Just Jake Pedlar, no other critter this early.'

'He comin' alone?'

'It's what he tol' me. His hoss been in for new plates. Jake's ridin' somewhere. He don't tell me where.'

'I'm gonna wait for him,' Harper said. 'You gonna give

me any trouble?'

'I ain't givin' nobody trouble, mister,' Wolf River Jack said. 'I just wanna say somethin'. You gonna hit me, do it on the right. Got kicked on the left by a mustang coupla years back, an' Doc Meeks, God rest his soul, told me another one there might finish me.'

Harper breathed in deeply. 'Stay outa the way, old man, an' you'll get no trouble.'

'I gotta open the big door behind you. Then I'll go an' keep the grullo company. She ain't been too good.'

'You can turn 'round.'

The liveryman turned slowly, his eyes widening as he saw Harper's face. 'Goddamn! You're that Harper feller!' His mouth closed like a rat-trap, as if wishing he hadn't said a word.

'Get the doors open, not too wide.' Harper ordered. 'I hear a noise outa you, it'll be your last.'

'Sure, sure! No trouble!'

Harper stood back as Wolf River Jack stepped past him to push up the heavy wooden bar holding the double doors. Moving quickly, he heaved back one door, swinging it back on well-oiled hinges maybe a couple of feet. With a hurried glance at Harper, he scuttled down the length of the barn to disappear beneath the neck of the grullo, the blue sheen of the animal's coat smooth in the lamplight.

Harper shifted to stand inside the barn, his back to the open door furthest from the light thrown by one of the oil lamps. Now came the hard part, waiting to find out if what Ruby Moreton had told him about Pedlar's plans for the morning was correct.

Not for the first time did he wonder how she managed to know so much of what was going on. Zeke had told him she rarely left the Golden Nugget. So, she was paying some-one for information. Pedlar's Frenchie barkeep, maybe?

George, or something like that. No, that's what Pedlar's men called him. Alphonse, that was it. The Frenchie, he remembered, had sounded more bitter than a little name-calling warranted.

The jingle of spurs and the impact of boots on the hardpack leading to the livery came to his ears. One man, alone. Harper pushed himself off the door, his Peacemaker held by the barrel, above shoulder height.

Pedlar stepped through the door. 'Wolf River Jack! You fixed them new plates like you been told?'

Harper brought down his sidearm, clipping the side of Pedlar's skull, careful not to make his strike too heavy. Pedlar stumbled, his legs sagging, and Harper jumped forward, one leg extended, kicking Pedlar onto the floor of the barn.

Dazed, Pedlar fell into the straw, face down, and Harper quickly straddled him, heaving Pedlar's sidearm into a pile of dung, running his hands over Pedlar, checking for hidden weapons. Satisfied, he stood up, walked back to close the door, and dropped the wooden bar.

He turned and raised his Peacemaker as Pedlar scrambled to his feet, his hand dropping to his side. Realizing he was unarmed, Pedlar's head jerked left and right, as if looking for a weapon.

'You move an inch, Pedlar, afore I say, an' I'm gonna shoot you down.'

'You're a dead man, Harper! I got three men comin' in after me!'

'No, you ain't,' Harper said evenly. He stared hard at Pedlar. 'You said you wanted another chance to kill me, now you got it. I never killed an unarmed man yet, Pedlar. But there's gotta be a first time. I reckon you know what really happened to Doc Meeks. An' you're gonna tell me.'

'You're crazy, Harper! I had nothin' to do with that!'

'That's what I'm gonna fmd out!'

In the lamplight, Pedlar's face showed the colour of congealed fat as Harper raised his sidearm. Then his expression changed, his eyes gleaming with hope, as Harper tossed the heavy weapon aside into the straw.

'You're no good to me dead, Pedlar. I'm gonna beat the truth out of your hide.'

Harper had barely finished his words when Pedlar let out a bull-like roar and, head down, he came down the barn like a human battering ram. His head smashed into Harper's chest, sending him flying back against a pile of hay to the side of one of the double doors.

Both men rolled around the ground, kicking and gouging, Pedlar attempting to rake his silver-slathered spurs the length of Harper's leg. Harper rolled away and gained purchase from one knee, drawing his left fist back shoulder high. As Pedlar rolled towards him, reaching out with outstretched arms, Harper smashed his fist into Pedlar's face, feeling the cheekbone collapse.

Pain shot through his arm from his clenched fist to his elbow, as he threw himself forward to grab Pedlar by the throat with both hands. Their faces were only inches apart, spittle flying from both men onto each other's faces. Pedlar grabbed at Harper's wrists, desperately pulling at each, attempting to break the hold. Unable to do so, his face turning purple as Harper increased the pressure, he pulled Harper towards him, shifting his body weight to bring his head lower in an attempt to smash his skull into Harper's face.

In an instant, Harper released his hold, rolled away across the barn, and jumped to his feet. His chest heaving, he sucked in air, sweat running down his face, blood dripping down his vest where one of Pedlar's spurs had raked his chin.

'We ain't finished yet, you murderin' sonovabitch!' Harper's eyes burned with fury. 'Doc Meeks, a good man! That trail-trash Clements! Two whores, or you know who did! Roper was shot an' coulda died!'

Pedlar, in the act of scrabbling to his feet, froze, his face a bloody mask turned upwards to Harper. 'Morgan ain't dead!'

'You had him strung up in that goddamned cage! An' fixed that note confessin' to killin' Doc Meeks!'

'What note? What the hell you talkin' 'bout? You got it wrong, Harper!'

Pedlar's face, one side livid with the mark of Harper's fist on his cheekbone, was screwed up with fury. 'I tried to bust him outa that cage! You know that!'

'Sure you did, to shut his mouth!'

Harper jumped forward, the strength of his arm brushing away Pedlar's attempt to defend himself, his fist sending Pedlar crashing to the ground.

Harper took a couple of paces back, his breathing heavy, rivulets of sweat running down his face.

'Get up you sonovabitch!'

Pedlar slowly began to clamber to his feet. His head rocking from side to side as if in denial of what Harper had said.

'Fer Chris'sakes, Harper! I wanted Morgan outa that jailhouse!'

Harper watched Pedlar carefully, as he stood, swaying gently, his head down, the fight appearing to have drained from him.

'Mr Harper!' Wolf River Jack called from down the barn.

'I told you to keep your mouth shut!'

'Mr Harper! I gotta tell you somethin': it's real important!'

134

Without turning his eyes away from Pedlar, Harper called out, 'I'm listenin'.'

'Jake wouldn't kill Morgan Clements!'

'Pedlar'd kill anybody to save his skin!'

'He'd not kill Morgan Clements. Morgan was Jake's boy, his only son!'

For a moment Harper was silent. 'You're lyin'!' he shouted. 'You're tryin' to save Pedlar's skin!'

'No, I ain't, Mr Harper.' The old liveryman's voice was confident. 'I been in Bridgetown since old Charlie Forrest was at the Double M, afore the miners came. Helped to bury Morgan's ma, Sarah Clements, when she died of mountain fever.'

'Doc Meeks was a good man.' Pedlar's voice was little more than a mumble now that the side of his face was ballooning. He lifted his head, still showing defiance. 'An' I know nothin' 'bout those whores!'

For a full half-minute Harper stared at Pedlar. Then he turned on his heel and picked up his Peacemaker from where it lay in the straw.

'You start trouble 'cross the bridge ever agin, an' I'll be back.'

Harper heaved open the door of the livery and stepped out into the morning light.

Harper was sipping steaming hot coffee from a tin cup, trying to ignore the pricking around his eyes caused by lack of sleep. He waited for Gladwin's response to what he'd just been told. The artist was deep in thought, staring sightlessly at the sketches spread out over the table at the end of the cabin they shared.

Finally Gladwin looked up, a frown on his face. 'You believed what Pedlar said?'

'The old liveryman convinced me. He was too quick

135

comin' up with Clements being Pedlar's son without it bein' true.'

'Pedlar might kill his own son to save himself.'

'You wouldn't say that if you'd seen Pedlar when I told him about Clements.'

Gladwin nodded thoughtfully. 'So! Dexter or Elliott!' His mouth set in firm line. 'Unless there's someone else we don't know about.'

Harper shook his head. 'Pedlar's been workin' for one of 'em. I'm damned sure of it. If I'd have had more time this mornin', I'd have kept goin' with Pedlar. Any longer, an' Jake's men might have turned up.'

Gladwin looked across the room through the window which overlooked the corral and the barn. 'Ah! More light on the problem! Maybe Sam has good news.'

Both men stood and went to the door, Harper opening it to see Sam Monroe hitching his horse to the rail.

'Howdy, Mr Harper, Mr Gladwin,' said the ex-soldier.

'C'm'on in, Sam. Coffee's hot.'

A rueful smile appeared on Sam's face. 'That's some good news, anyways.'

Harper and Gladwin exchanged glances.

The three men went into the cabin, Sam helping himself from the pot which bubbled away on the stove.

'I did what you tol' me, Mr Harper. There ain't a nook or cranny over the bridge that I ain't seen these last few days. But no sightin' of that Cap'n Elliott. Seems like the feller's lit outa town.'

'You reckon it's worth goin' back?'

'No, sir, I don't. I talked to—' Monroe stopped suddenly, peering down the length of the cabin.

'What is it, Sam?' Gladwin asked.

Monroe turned to Harper. 'You ain't playin' games with me, Mr Harper?'

'What you talkin' 'bout, Sam?'

Monroe pointed to the papers pinned to the wall above the table where Gladwin worked each morning. 'You got me searchin' for Cap'n Elliott, an' all the time you got a picture of him here.'

'Sam, that's Mr Gladwin's drawing of Jake Pedlar. Take my word. Pedlar could never have been an officer in the 54th!'

'No, Mr Harper! I know that's Jake Pedlar. I seen him lotsa times these last days. I'm talkin' about the other picture. That one of Cap'n Elliott!' Harper and Gladwin stared across the cabin to where the pencil sketch was tacked to the wall alongside the one of Pedlar.

'My God!' Gladwin said. 'That's one I drew of Clay Dexter!'

Harper and Sam Monroe reined in and slid from their saddles to hitch their mounts to the rail outside Bolden's office. From the moment Monroe had recognized that Clay Dexter and Elliott were one and the same, Harper had moved fast. Knowing that Joe Jessop was away in Cheyenne he'd ordered Tom Gladwin and Zeke to stand guard at the Double M. First he and Monroe had mustered all the spare ammunition they could find. Then, taking fresh horses from the barn they'd ridden them hard from the Double M into Bridgetown.

Harper went up the steps two at a time, Monroe close behind him, and threw open the door. Opposite, Bolden and Frank Jackson were taking long guns down from the gunrack. Bolden scarcely looked up from loading a Winchester.

'Seems we gotta habit of meetin' at the right time, Luke!' Bolden said, half over his shoulder. 'I'm sure glad to see you!'

'Dexter's the killer!' Harper said. 'He's a renegade army officer name of Elliott!'

'I ain't got time for that now! Feller ridin' through tells me there's a goddamned war goin' over at Dexter's spread! Jake Pedlar's tryin' to kill 'em all.'

'You ain't gonna try an' stop it?'

Bolden looked up, his large teeth showing. 'I ain't that crazy! But if anyone's walkin' when it's over, I'm plannin' to throw 'em in jail! Might even clean up this town first week I'm here!'

Bolden took up a key and locked the guncase. 'You both ready to move?'

Harper's face set. 'That's why we're in Bridgetown! I got a debt to settle!'

CHAPTER FOURTEEN

'I've ridden this land before,' Harper explained. 'Dexter's big house is beyond that ridge.' He pointed northwards to rising land, maybe half a mile away. 'We'll be lookin' down on it from the high point. The house is maybe five hundred yards on from the ridge.'

He frowned, looking around at Bolden. 'You sure that feller ridin' through was straight? Seems damned quiet for what he was tellin' you.'

Harper reined in his mount, bringing the animal down to a walk, the other three matching the pace. Bolden reached down and took out his Winchester.

'You think we're ridin' into a trap?'

'Not unless they're flat down beyond the ridge with no horses,' Harper said. 'I got the fastest horse. You fellers stay here, an' I'll take a look.'

Without waiting for an answer he spurred his horse forward, galloping towards the ridge, and pulling his Winchester from its sheath as he approached the high point. Ten yards from the ridge, his thighs locked onto the horse's sides, keeping him solid in the saddle as he brought up the long gun ready to fire should anyone be waiting beyond the ridge.

He breathed in deeply, feeling his muscles tense. Ten more yards and he'd be looking down on the big house. The big horse reached the crest of the ridge, and Harper let out an oath as his hand dropped away from supporting the barrel of his Winchester to take up the reins.

'For the love of God!'

Below him, for fifty yards around the entrance to the house the ground was littered with the bodies of fallen men. Some were stretched out on open ground, some half over the low wall which ran in front of the house. Other bodies could be seen on the tops of mounds of hay. Near a barn, a man sat on the ground, his legs stretched out, holding his head from which blood poured. Close to him the bodies of a woman and a young boy lay motionless.

On the steps leading to the door of the house sat what looked like a young child, hands together in an attitude of prayer. Beside her, the body of a woman was face down, her voluminous skirts soaked with blood, scrunched up to show her legs. To the right of her body, lay the carcasses of three horses, one of them a big roan.

Harper turned in his saddle and waved the three riders forward, turning back to keep watch on the scene below, checking that the only sign of movement was from the man by the barn who was now beginning to slide away into the dirt, his hands still held to his head.

'Fer Chris'sakes, Luke!' Bolden said, as he reined in alongside, surveying the scene below.

'You think anyone's alive?' Monroe asked.

'One way to find out,' said Harper. He raised his Winchester, and taking careful aim, put a shot into the wood to the side of the door of the house. Nothing moved. Neither the child by the house nor the man near the barn showed any sign that they'd heard the shot.

SHADOW OF THE GUN

'We gotta get that child,' Bolden said. 'We're goin' down.'

Harper slid his Winchester into its sheath, drew his Peacemaker, and urged his mount forward. The four riders, line abreast, held their mounts to a slow walk as they approached the house, their eyes constantly shifting to and fro. Harper looked down carefully as they passed each body. There was no sign of Dexter, dead or alive.

As they got closer they could hear sobbing. Loud gasps rent the air as breath was sucked in and expelled.

'Mister! Mister! Help me!'

'That ain't a child, that's a gel!' Frank said.

Harper leapt to the ground. What he thought was an attitude of prayer was in fact the girl's hands bound tightly together. She was young and thin, wearing only a thin shift, torn at the shoulders. Her skin showed the blue-red stripes of a whipping.

Harper pulled out a knife and cut through the ropes.

'You're safe now,' he said.

She turned her face upwards and he saw the knife scar on the underside of her jaw and recognized the young Jeannie who had approached him the first time he'd called on Ruby Moreton.

'You're alive, be thankful,' he said. 'Where's Dexter?'

At the mention of Dexter's name the girl's eyes bulged with fear, her whole body trembling, and she began to sob even louder than before.

'Look after her, Frank.'

A knife in one hand, his Peacemaker in the other, Harper went up the steps and through the doorway into the hall of the house. Surveying the scene, he swallowed rapidly a couple of times. Another time, another place, and this could have been the aftermath of a Comanche attack. Blood was sprayed over the floor, across the furniture, and against the walls. Many of the men who lay dead outside must have been hit here, and lived long enough to attempt an escape.

Three of them didn't make it, their bodies, almost in a straight line, were stretched across the polished boards of the floor. A glance told Harper that not one of the bodies was Dexter's.

Then Harper saw the spurs slathered with silver.

Sheathing his knife, Harper stepped across the hall to fall to one knee alongside Jake Pedlar. He grasped one shoulder, and turned Pedlar over. Blood oozed from a chest wound, trickling onto Pedlar's leather vest. His heart was pumping. Pedlar was still alive.

'Pedlar! It's Harper! Where's Dexter?'

Pedlar's eyes remained closed, his breath shallow, tiny bubbles of blood flecking his lips. His lungs were shredded, Harper knew. Pedlar would be dead in ten minutes.

'He killed your son, Jake! I'll kill Dexter for you! Where is he, Jake?'

Pedlar's eyelids fluttered, before his eyes opened fully. 'He killed my boy.'

His voice was weak, and Harper strained forward to hear him. 'Where's Dexter gone, Jake?' Harper said urgently.

Pedlar attempted to speak, the bubbles of blood on his lips deepening in colour.

'Jake! Listen to me! Dexter! I gotta find Dexter!'

Harper was aware that Bolden and the others had come into the hall behind him. He turned around, aware that desperation must have been showing in his eyes. Conscious of their stares, he ignored them and turned back to Pedlar. If John Meeks was to have justice, even after death, then Pedlar was going to tell him where Dexter had gone.

'Try Jake, try! Dexter killed your son. Where did he go?'

Pedlar, his eyes unfocused now, his life fading behind the mist which blurred his eyes, appeared to make one last physical effort, grasping at Harper's hand which had remained clutched to Pedlar's shoulder.

'He's gone for your woman, Harper.' His voice was surprisingly strong. 'Kill the sonovabitch for both of us!'

Pedlar fell back, and with a final prolonged expulsion of air that sprayed blood across the polished boards, ceased to breathe.

Harper, his feet hard against his irons, his head low over his horse's neck that was covered in white foam, rounded the final bend bringing the side of the Double M house into view. He urged the exhausted animal into even greater effort with a cruel dig of his spurs into the animal's sides.

Icy fingers clutched at his insides. If Dexter had harmed Abby he'd flay the bastard alive, until he screamed for release. He turned the animal's head to skirt the barn, and the horse swerved as it reached the man face down in the dirt.

'Goddamnit to hell!'

Harper swore as he recognized Zeke. He heaved on his reins bringing the animal back onto the beaten earth, and urged the animal forward.

'Abby! Abby!' Harper shouted, as he raced around the corral. He could see her green dress on the steps of the house! He hauled back on the reins, jumping from the saddle as he reached it.

Abby sat on the steps, cradling Tom Gladwin's head in her lap. Blood from his shoulder had soaked her skirts, the soft material stiff with gore. The Englishman's face was ashen, his eyes closed, his back resting against the two lowest steps, his long legs sprawling lifelessly in the dirt.

Terror marked Abby's face, high red spots prominent against the flour-white complexion of her face.

'He's taken Charlie!' she screamed. She held up a hand to point beyond the corral. 'Maybe ten minutes ago!'

'Zeke's horse! Is it in the barn?'

'Yes, yes! Go, Luke!' Her head fell forward, choking sobs forcing themselves from deep inside her.

'I'll bring him back, Abby!'

Harper swung on his heel, already aware that he'd uttered words that one day might come back to haunt him. He raced across to his horse and grabbed his Winchester, then ran to the barn, dust kicking up from his boots, his spurs ringing. He could be in for a long ride. It was too risky to chase Dexter riding bare-back. If Zeke had already saddled his palomino he had a chance of catching Dexter. If not, he could only hope for a short chase.

He ran through the open doorway of the barn, and was blinded momentarily by his swift transition from the afternoon sun into the shadows. Impatiently, he waited the couple of seconds until his eyes cleared. Yes! Zeke's palomino, already saddled, stood loosely hitched to an iron ring, its jaws working steadily at a morral.

Harper ran forward and tossed Zeke's Springfield away, sheathing his Winchester. He ripped away the morral, threw it into a corner and, clutching the reins, ran the horse the length of the barn and into the light. Briefly raising his arm in the direction of Abby, and not sure whether she saw his salute, he flung himself into the saddle, turned the animal's head, and spurred the horse forward.

'You'd better be as goddamned fast as Zeke said!' Harper said aloud.

Clear of the barn, Harper allowed the horse to settle down into a steady lope. There'd be time for a faster pace if and when he caught up with Dexter. Or Elliott, or whatever the devil's real name was.

What was that saying that he'd once heard Tom Gladwin use? 'The gods move in mysterious ways.' That was it. Pedlar, the very man Dexter had hired to do his dirty work, had finally been the cause of bringing him down. Dexter, Harper realized, could never have known that Clements was Pedlar's son.

Now Dexter was looking only for a way out, aiming to ride out of the territory with his hostage as far as he could reach before Harper, or the law, caught up with him. Had he promised Abby he'd let Charlie go? His eyes scanning the horizon, Harper shook his head as if a rider alongside him had asked a question. When he was clear, Dexter would kill Charlie. Men like Dexter knew no mercy.

A speck of colour moved on the horizon.

Harper scrabbled behind him. Did Zeke carry a spyglass? Yes! Harper's gloved fingers grasped the brass tube and heaved, at the same time reining in the palomino to a halt. He was gambling valuable time, he knew. He raised the spyglass to his eye, giving a quick turn of the barrel to bring the speck of colour into focus. Harper's face creased into a grim smile of satisfaction. Two figures sat astride one horse, the animal progressing at a lope. Dexter and Charlie!

His mind went back to when he was out here searching for the Monument plants. That was it! Dexter had to cross the river. At this time of the year there was only one safe place to cross. Dexter would know it, but so did he. He rammed the spyglass back into the saddle-bag, and picked up the rein. He leaned forward to tug at the animal's ear.

'You got some hard ridin' now,' he said aloud.

He touched his spurs into the animal's sides, more confident now that he could see his quarry and was able to work out where Dexter was going. The animal broke from a lope into a gallop, its nostrils dilating, and its mane stirring in the breeze. Chips of flint and spurts of dust sprayed from its hoofs as Harper, leaning forward, his eyes on the figures in the distance, urged the animal to ever greater speed.

Within a few minutes Harper was aware that the gap was closing. Dexter appeared unaware that he was being pursued for his animal maintained a steady lope. For a moment Harper thought of reaching for his Winchester when in range, but quickly dismissed the idea. He couldn't risk hitting Charlie. He had to close in, and hope there was some way he could free the boy before tackling Dexter.

The distance had now closed. What was once a speck on the horizon had cleared to be recognizable figures, Dexter back in the saddle, Charlie held before him. Beyond them Harper caught a glimpse of the river, a thin blue band sparkling in the sun.

Dexter must have reined in his mount, as Harper saw the animal halt, the distance between the horses beginning to close rapidly. Zeke's horse, blowing hard, covered the ground with long strides.

Dexter's horse suddenly leapt forward. Harper had been spotted. His hand dropped to the stock of his Winchester. Dare he try to put a slug into Dexter's horse?

'Too damned dangerous!' Harper said aloud, through gritted teeth.

But he was closing the gap. Dexter's horse, slowed by the extra weight, was no match for the palomino ridden by Harper. Now the river was only a few hundred yards away.

And Harper saw a way of freeing Charlie.

He knew he had to judge his moment. Too early and Charlie would be seriously injured if not killed. Too late, and Dexter would have regained control of both his horse and of Charlie. Much depended on the boy. Was he aware that Dexter was being pursued? Would the boy's natural fear of Dexter prevent him from reacting?

Slowing his own mount, accepting that he was falling behind Dexter again, Harper stood up in his irons to watch for exactly the right moment. There! Dexter's horse hesitated momentarily at the bank of the river, until spurred forward by Dexter. Then the animal plunged into the swirling water.

Harper let out a piercing whistle.

There was a brief tussle between man and boy before Charlie threw himself from the saddle, hitting the surface of the river with a great cascade of water. For two long seconds he disappeared beneath the waters but to Harper's relief, his head finally surfaced and he began to swim strongly for the bank.

Dexter jerked his head around as if to judge the distance between himself and Harper. As if aware for the first time of how close Harper was he ducked his head down beside the horse's neck. The animal, its head back, swam strongly for the opposite bank.

Harper raced his horse forward, unsheathing his Winchester, as he reined in at the river-bank. Steadying himself in the saddle he raised the long gun to his shoulder. From this range he couldn't miss.

'Help me! Help me!'

Harper looked around, away from the long gun. Hell! Charlie was twenty yards from the bank, his arm held high. A second later, he disappeared from view, before surfacing once more, his choking voice now unable to be heard by Harper.

Harper snapped the long gun back in its sheath. He rode his horse forward ten yards into the water, already reaching for the tie securing Zeke's thirty foot of hemp.

Whirling the rope, he hurled the loop to land it across the boy's shoulders. He turned the palomino's head, and hauled the spluttering, choking Charlie onto the bank.

'I'll be back, Charlie!'

Harper threw away the rope, once more spurring his horse forward into the water, as he saw Dexter reach the opposite bank. Would Dexter wait calmly and try to pick him off as he crossed the river? He drew his Peacemaker and fired a shot. His chances of hitting Dexter at this range, he knew were slight, but he might prevent Dexter from standing his ground.

He fired again, and by luck dirt close to Dexter's horse spurted skywards. Dexter turned his horse's head and urged the animal up the bank away from the river. Two minutes later, Harper was doing the same, his Peacemaker back in its holster, Dexter maybe a quarter a mile ahead of him.

But the chase had been too much for Dexter's horse, and Harper could see the distance closing at every stride of the palomino. There was a rush of air close to him, immediately followed by the crack of a rifle shot.

Goddamnit! He reached for the Winchester, raised it to his shoulder, firing and levering as fast as he could, his legs solid against the horse's sides, keeping his aim steady as he charged down on Dexter. He felt a sudden rush of air pass close to his face, and an instant later the sound of Dexter's rifle. Frantically, he levered the Winchester. Two more shots and he'd have to reach for his Peacemaker. He levered the last slug and suddenly, Dexter's horse reared, its hoofs pawing at the air. There was an instant when the animal, still with Dexter in the saddle, appeared to be suspended in the late afternoon light.

Harper heard a human scream of fear as the horse fell

back, blood spraying over Dexter, the weight of the horse crushing the man against the hard ground. The animal gave one final jerk and rolled, its hoofs pointing skywards. Dexter lay face upwards, his skull crushed, his eyes open, unaware of the light rain that had begun to fall, and the figure of Harper, Peacemaker in hand, looking down at him from the saddle of the palomino.

CHAPTER FIFTEEN

Abigail Forrest raised the crystal glass and took a small sip of the red wine. 'You're not wearing your blue bandanna today,' she said.

Harper smiled. He knew she was being playful with him, and it didn't bother him at all. 'I arrive in Boston in trail clothes and those cousins of mine will reckon a Wild West cowboy and a coupla longhorns are joinin' the family!'

He smoothed the material of his coat with one hand. 'Feller from the dry goods store got back from Cheyenne coupla days ago. He's done a good job.'

Abby's eyes shone. 'Dark-blue coat, blue vest, silk shirt, grey trousers, new hand-tooled boots! He certainly has!'

'And don't forget the cream Stetson in the hall.'

She laughed aloud. 'Goodness, we mustn't forget the hat!'

She glanced up at the mahogany-cased wall clock.

'Joe Jessop wants to see me. Do you know what it's about?'

Harper shook his head, but before he had chance to reply there was a knock at the door. Abby's girl opened it.

'Mr Jessop,' she said.

'Don't forget me, Maria!' Zeke exclaimed, as the two men entered the room.

'Howdy, Miss Abby!'

'Joe, Zeke,' Abby greeted them.

'How's the head?' Harper asked Zeke.

'Better every day, Mr Harper.' Zeke's face split with a broad grin. 'Mr Jessop says it's a good job I've a thick skull.'

'You wanted to see me, Joe?'

Jessop nodded, shifting his feet awkwardly. 'Kinda tricky, Miss Abby.'

Abby smiled. 'Joe, you've been with the Double M for over thirty years. Be as tricky as you wish!'

'Well, that's just it, Miss Abby.' His eyes shifted from her to Zeke and back again. 'You see, me and Zeke, well, we're quittin' the Double M.'

Abby's mouth formed a perfect circle. 'Oh,' she said. She glanced at Harper before looking back at the two men.

Zeke stepped forward. 'Mr Jessop ain't tellin' this right,' he said. 'Fact is, Miss Abby, I'm gonna be your neighbour! My ma's bought the Dexter place now she's sold the Golden Nugget.'

Again Abby's mouth formed a perfect circle. She turned her astonished gaze towards Harper, seeking support.

'Ruby Moreton's your mother?' Harper said.

'Sure is, Mr Harper. I never tol' nobody 'cos that's what she wanted.' Zeke stood up proudly. 'She tol' me it's time she got back to bein' a decent widder-woman.'

Joe Jessop ran his fingers around the edge of his hat. 'Zeke's gonna need a lotta help gettin' the place started agin, Miss Abby. So I jest . . .' His voice trailed away.

Abby clapped her hands together in delight. 'It's a wonderful idea, Zeke! And how lucky you are to have Joe to help. When the men get back from the railhead we'll talk about stock.'

The two men exchanged relieved grins. 'That's mighty

151

generous of you, Miss Abby,' Zeke said. His expression became serious. 'Maria tells me you're gonna see Mr Gladwin after you've seen the sheriff. If it hadn't been for Mr Gladwin I guess I wouldn't be standin' here. Me and Mr Jessop, well, jest tell Mr Gladwin we hope he makes it.'

'I'll do that, Zeke. We gotta hope he's lucky,' Harper said. He frowned as a thought came to him. 'Dexter's backers in England didn't try to stop the sale of the ranch?'

And, as he and Abby listened to what Zeke had to say, Harper began to realize how close Dexter had been to achieving his aims.

Bolden was caught so unawares that he almost spilled his coffee over Harper. He swung around to Abby who was sitting on the high-backed chair beneath the gunrack in his office.

'Now ain't that somethin'! Who's Zeke's ma bought it from?'

'Walter Riley's kinfolk back East. Dexter only ever made one payment, promising them he'd settle when he could sell cattle.'

Bolden frowned. 'What about these rich folks back in England?'

'They never existed,' Abby said. 'Dexter used them as an excuse to stand back. At the same time he was paying Pedlar to raid the Double M intending to buy it when I threw in my hand.'

Bolden bared his large teeth. 'Man made a mistake there, Miss Abby.' He grunted loudly. 'That Dexter sure was a sidewinder.'

'I think John Meeks gave him a chance,' Harper said. 'A doctor knows what War can do to a man. But when the first girl was murdered, and John couldn't trust the sheriff, he wrote for my help.'

'You think Doc Meeks was tol' something?'

Harper nodded. 'I reckon the girl Janey gave him the cameo belonging to Bella that Doc Scott found. Although after Janey disappeared what led him to try and find where she was buried, I guess we'll never know.'

'Me an' Frank gonna go out there next week, have a look 'round. Give the gal a proper burial. Miss Morris'll want to know what we've done.' Bolden snapped his fingers, remembering something. 'Got a message on the stage, from South Pass. Miss Morris'll not be here for another four weeks. You've another month o' studying, Miss Abby!'

Abby smiled but shook her head. 'Studying will have to wait, Mr Bolden. I'm leaving for Boston in a couple of days.'

Bolden was silent for a moment, obviously surprised, looking first at Abby and then at Harper. Realization showed slowly in his eyes. His large teeth flashed a big smile across the desk.

'This sure is a mornin' for surprises! An' I'm bettin' I got it right! Ain't this the best news I've heard for a time!' He looked across at his deputy. 'Me an' Frank better get some decent clothes to come callin'!'

Harper stood up, aware that a sheepish grin was across his face. 'Doc Scott says we need to see Tom Gladwin afore we leave. We're off to see him now.'

Bolden nodded. 'Let's hope he's as lucky as that cowhand.' He turned to Abby. 'You mind if I have a word just with Luke, Miss Abby?'

'I'll wait in the buggy, Luke,' she said, the men getting to their feet as she stood up.

Bolden waited until she had closed the door. He rubbed his large knuckles across his mouth as if unsure how to begin.

'You're a lucky man, Luke, but you know that. I guess Miss Abby's tol' you about Walter Riley's son?'

Harper nodded. 'He almost ruined the Double M when they were married. I'm told you were sheriff when he shot himself in Plainsville.'

Bolden looked across at his deputy before looking back to face Harper.

'That's what I tol' folks, Miss Abby wantin' to go for the law. Truth is, Riley an' two others tried to rob the stage. Only me and Frank was onboard comin' back from Cheyenne, so they all got what was comin' to 'em. After that, Miss Abby dug up some fancy law and got the Forrest name back for herself an' young Charlie.'

Again Bolden glanced across at his deputy before looking back at Harper. 'Frank's had things to tell me. Fact is, we aim to be 'round these parts for a while, an' now I guess you're gonna be here as well. Best if we all start off right an' proper.'

'I'm obliged to you, William,' Harper said. 'Best if some things are forgotten.' He turned to Jackson. 'Good to hear you ain't quittin', Frank. Town needs a good deputy. Bring Lucy out to the Double M sometime.'

Jackson's face lit up. 'I'll do that, Mr Harper.'

'We'll be back in a month,' Harper said.

Bolden gave a mock grimace. 'Take your time. Reckon this town's gonna be kinda quiet now you've gone back to bein' a city gent.' He pretended to peer closely at Harper's hip. 'Though I 'spect, Luke, if I looked in that buggy outside I'd find that cannon o' yourn!'

As the buggy made its way along Main Street it seemed to Harper they could barely travel ten yards before some man or woman hailed them from the boardwalk.

'The town's a changed place,' Abby said. 'I haven't seen

154

people this happy for many months.'

Harper had to agree. The grim expressions of the townspeople he'd first encountered on his arrival in Bridgetown had been replaced with smiling faces. Even a couple of miners, across from the other side of the bridge, held up their hands in greeting.

Harper turned the buggy leading to Dr Scott's house, and was securing the pony when Scott appeared at the doorway.

'Mr Harper! Miss Abby!' Scott called. 'Have you heard the good news?'

'I guess you're about to tell us, Doc!'

Harper turned back to push his gunbelt further beneath the buggy seat.

Then, with Abby's hand on his arm, he entered the doctor's house.

'Mr Miller from the bank returned from Cheyenne on the stage an hour ago. Union Pacific are planning to build a spur to Bridgetown.'

'That's great news, Doc.' He glanced at Abby, to see her attempting to stifle a smile.

'We need to see Tom Gladwin.'

Scott looked thoughtful. 'Erm, Miss Abby. . . ?'

'Tom Gladwin saved my life, Doctor. I'll not be shocked by seeing him in bed.'

'No, of course you'll not.'

Scott led the way into his house and to the room where Harper had spoken with the cowboy Dan Roper. They paused at the door, and behind Scott, Abby held out her hand and squeezed Harper's fingers.

Scott opened the door. Gladwin occupied the same bed once taken by Roper. He was propped against the pillows, his face pale, his eyes closed.

'Mr Gladwin,' Scott said softly. 'You have visitors.'

Gladwin's eyes snapped open, light gleaming in his black pupils.

'Luke! Miss Abby!'

Harper felt the tension drain away. Beside him, Abby gave a long sigh. She crossed to the bed, reaching out a hand to rest it briefly on Gladwin's arm. 'It's good to see you getting better, Tom,' she said.

Harper grinned at the artist. 'Luck's with you, Tom.'

'Not luck at all, Mr Harper!' Scott exclaimed.

A smile lit up his face. 'That packet you brought for John and gave to me. Have you any idea what was in it?'

Harper shook his head. 'Something for doctorin', I was told.'

Scott leaned forward, his eyes shining with enthusiasm.

'Something for doctoring, indeed, Mr Harper! A great man in England, by the name of Joseph Lister, has discovered how we can stop gunshot wounds festering. No! Not just gunshot wounds, all wounds! I've read the notes you brought. I've tried what Lister has said. The problem is not with the air around the wound, as we've been thinking, the festering is started by the flesh itself. Carbolic is the cure, Mr Harper! It works, it works!'

Harper hastily suppressed a smile. Scott's enthusiasm had caused him to knock over the small inkpot on the table, and the doctor was hastily dabbing at the black liquid while shooting looks of triumph at Harper.

'I can still draw, so that means I'll be able to paint!' Gladwin exclaimed. He stared at Harper as if seeing him for the first time.

'Excellent! Luke, you look quite the dandy.'

Harper grinned. 'Maybe I should have stuck to trail clothes. I'm dressed to go back to Boston in a coupla days.'

'Are you staying long?'

Harper smiled, 'We'll be back in a month.'

Swift understanding shone in Gladwin's eyes but before he could say a word Scott clapped his hand to his fore-head.

'I almost forgot! I've a letter from Boston just in from the stage.' He reached into an inside pocket of his jacket and took out a long sealed package. He looked at Harper.

'You knew John well, I guess. I think I should open it now.'

Without waiting for an answer, he carefully unsealed the package and took out a letter. Large letters at the top of the paper, visible to them all, made it appear important.

Scott scanned the letter. 'Yes, this is it,' he said. He hummed to himself softly, apparently missing out words he considered unimportant. 'Ah! Here it is. *"We are urgently attempting to contact Doctor John Mark Meeks's sole heir. This is proving difficult as Mr—"* '

Scott broke off suddenly, his eyebrows knitting together in apparent confusion. 'I don't understand. . . .'

'The waiting is agony, Dr Scott,' Tom Gladwin said. 'Please read on.'

' *"This is proving difficult as the whereabouts of his sole heir are uncertain at the time of writing. Mr Lucas Matthew Harper has recently resigned from the Boston branch of the Pinkerton Detective Agency and is known only to have travelled somewhere to the West".*' He looked up, eyebrows raised in astonish-ment.

'Tom was my only stepbrother,' Harper said quietly. Unconsciously, his fingers brushed the beaver pin fastened beneath his jacket. 'Same mother, different fathers. John wrote and said he desperately needed my help.' His mouth twisted. 'I was too late.'

Scott looked first at Gladwin then at Abigail Forrest, and then back to Harper.

'Maybe you were too late to save John, but you've saved

Bridgetown,' the doctor said firmly. 'John's great wish, he spoke to me of it many times, was that the town and all the decent people here would prosper. Now, due to your courage, they will.'

'Doctor Scott's right, Luke,' Abby said. 'And you saved the Double M. John Meeks would have been proud of you. And so am I.'

'A portrait of you both!' Gladwin exclaimed. 'Free of charge!'

The Englishman must have seen the light in Abby's eyes as she looked up at Harper and placed her hand on his arm.

'Dash!' Gladwin exclaimed in mock despair. 'I should have charged a large fee.' He pushed himself off his pillows. 'I'll make it a wedding present! On one condition! I insist on being Luke's groomsman!'

Harper threw back his head and laughed aloud, his hand closing over that of Abby's. 'We agree, Tom! Just promise you'll not wear that crazy suit!'